A Victorian Rose

A VICTORIAN ROSE

CATHERINE PALMER

TYNDALE HOUSE PUBLISHERS, INC., WHEATON, ILLINOIS

Library of Congress Cataloging-in-Publication Data

Palmer, Catherine
  Victorian rose / Catherine Palmer.
    p. cm.
  ISBN 0-8423-1957-3 (alk. paper)
  I. Yorkshire (England)—Fiction. 2. Pro-life movement—Fiction. 3. Physicians—Fiction.
4. Widows—Fiction. I. Title.
  PS3566.A495 V54 2002
813'.54—dc21   2002004451

Printed in the United States of America

08 07 06 05 04 03 02
9   8   7   6   5   4   3   2   I

To Maria Hines
WITH GRATITUDE AND LOVE

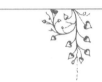

Acknowledgments

My DEEP THANKS to my neighbor and friend, Maria Hines, for discovering and teaching me about *Helleborus niger,* the Christmas Rose. May God reward you for your boundless enthusiasm for this project and for your dedication in locating so much valuable information for me.

I wish also to thank Raoul Guise of Otley, England, for bringing your little town to life so vividly in my mind. Thank you for your hours of photocopying and e-mailing, and for your patience in answering my many questions.

Of course, the gentle hand of my editor is always greatly valued. Thank you, Kathy Olson, for your tender shaping and pruning of this manuscript. And to the HeartQuest and Women's Fiction team, God bless you!

ONE

LONGLEY PARK CONSERVATORY
OTLEY, YORKSHIRE—1839

"IT REFUSES TO BLOOM!" Clementine Laird glared at the leathery evergreen leaves of a small potted plant. "Why will it not produce any flowers for me, Mr. Hedgley? I have done all I can to coax it, coddle it, everything but tuck it into bed at night. Yet it sits there staring at me as though it has no intention of ever making a blossom—and all just to spite me."

The old man's smile widened the wreath of wrinkles lining his weathered face. "It ain't time for t' Christmas Rose to bloom, Mrs. Laird," he said, giving the terra-cotta pot a turn. "It's barely November, and t' old girl don't usually set flowers till late January or February. Ye cannot 'urry a beautiful thing, me dear."

"But I must hurry it!" Clemma set her hands on her hips and peered intently into the foliage, hoping to spot a bud. "I cannot exhibit my paintings unless I have a Christmas Rose among them. It is not enough to show holly and ivy, Mr. Hedgley. I must have a December flower, and the only one that blooms in that month is *Helleborus niger*—the Christmas Rose."

"She don't 'ardly never bloom in December, me dear lady. I done told ye that near onto fifty times, I reckon."

"But I have brought this plant inside the conservatory." Clemma spread her arms to encompass the vast glass-and-iron hall filled with ferns, bamboos, citrus trees, philodendrons, and other exotic plants. Surely such a living, warm, and very green place should lure the *Helleborus* blossoms out of hiding.

"Indeed ye 'ave, but flowers listen to God more often than they listen to us. Can ye not recall t' words of Solomon? 'To every thing there is a season, and a time to every purpose under t' 'eaven: A time to be born, and a time to die; a time to plant, and a time to pluck up that which is planted.' Ye know them words as good as I do. And t' ones that follow 'em: ''e 'ath made every thing beautiful in 'is time.'"

"Yes, but—"

"'ose time?"

"His time. God's time. Yes, I know, I know."
Clemma let out a breath of resignation and turned
away from the uncooperative plant. "But if that
naughty *Helleborus* has failed to bloom by Christmas
Eve, then I shall be forced to title my exhibition
something other than 'A Year of Flowers in
Yorkshire,' and I shall be severely annoyed. Did
I tell you, Mr. Hedgley, that I have invited the
renowned publisher, Mr. Street, to come to Otley
all the way from London? He has seen my other
paintings and is quite interested in this collection.
I have great hope that my work finally may be made
into a book."

"Aye, ye 'ave told me," he said. "Frequently."

Clemma seated herself at a table upon which
she had gathered a collection of late autumn
flora—chrysanthemums, asters, rose hips, and ears
of ripe wheat. Although she had planned to paint
each month's flowers at the height of their bloom,
in midsummer she had fallen behind schedule.
Now the chrysanthemums were past their prime,
and the asters had begun to droop. She must get
them into water immediately or her entire project
was likely to wilt as well.

"Will you stay to tea, Mr. Hedgley?" she asked
as she began stripping away dead leaves. "I expect it
will be brought down from the great house at any
moment. You are more than welcome to join me."

"Nay, but thank ye, Mrs. Laird, for I must be gettin' back to me own cottage lest Mrs. 'edgley give me a piece of 'er mind. Farewell, then."

"Good afternoon, Mr. Hedgley."

Clemma hardly noticed the old man as he moved down the path inside the conservatory. Absorbed in arranging the asters in a vase, she felt a flutter of panic in her stomach. This exhibition of her art was the most important thing to happen to her in many years, and she was determined to make it a success.

Raised near the little Yorkshire town of Otley, she had always dreamed of sailing the seven seas, riding horseback across the American frontier, bowing before Indian maharajas, and finding the source of the Nile. But at her father's insistence, she had followed the example of her three elder sisters and married young. It was a blessed union, for not only had Clemma loved Thomas Laird, but marrying him had made her the mistress of a fine manor and the wife of a wealthy man. Not a full year into the marriage, however, their grand home was struck by lightning. It caught fire and burned to the ground. Thomas perished in the blaze.

Clemma, who was badly injured, had deeply mourned the death of her young husband. She moved back to the family home of Brooking House to recover, and slowly she assumed full care for her aging parents. Somehow, in the years that drifted by, her dreams of adventure and passion faded. She took lessons in the art school housed at nearby Longley Park, and she spent most of her time painting flowers inside the great conservatory. Now, at thirty-two, she knew she would never remarry, and she was far too settled to explore Africa or sail away to India. She was, she realized, a bit dull.

Gazing at the chrysanthemums she had placed in the vase with the asters, she leaned her elbows on the table and rested her chin in her hands. Dull. Dispirited. Boring. How had she withered away to such a pale vestige of her former self? How had she let herself become so . . .

"No!" she cried out, slapping her hands down on the table and pushing herself up. She would not succumb to this spirit of defeat that assailed her. Grasping a stick of charcoal, she turned to her easel and began to sketch the outline of the simple glass vase. God had blessed her with a good life, and she was a happy woman. She needed nothing, no one.

"Excuse me, miss!"

The voice came from the far end of the conservatory. It was the footman with the tea.

"Put it on the small table in the niche near the palm trees," Clemma called. "I do hope you warmed the milk this time."

"I beg your pardon?"

She glanced around the frame of her canvas at the footman. Tall and broad shouldered, he stared at her with icy blue eyes. Why was he not wearing his livery? Clemma wondered as she stepped out from behind the easel. And where was the tea tray?

"Did you say something about milk?" he asked, starting down the path toward her. She could see now that the man was not as young as she first had supposed, for his dark brown hair was threaded with silver, and subtle lines softened the outer corners of his eyes. Moreover, he did not look much like a footman. Wearing a long black frock coat with velvet cuffs, he sported an embroidered waistcoat of indigo blue and a silk cravat.

"Milk," she repeated, feeling a little off balance. "Indeed, I thought you had come about the tea."

"No . . . oranges, to be exact. Oranges and lemons."

"Oranges?" Her focus darted to the double rows of orange trees hanging heavy with fruit. "What can you mean, sir?"

"I wish to purchase a dozen oranges. I should be pleased to take several lemons as well. And some limes, if you have them."

"Goodness, I mistook you for the footman!" she said, feeling a flush of heat pour into her cheeks. "Not that you resemble a servant, of course, for you are clearly a gentleman, and . . . that is . . . we normally do not sell the fruit grown in the conservatory . . . sir."

"What becomes of it?"

"The kitchens use it in providing meals for the art students who have taken residence at Longley Park."

"Am I to assume you are one of these students?"

He glanced at her easel, and Clemma felt intense gratitude that it was turned the wrong way around. For some reason, this man disconcerted her, and she was not sure why. He was certainly handsome, and he displayed the elegance and mannerisms of a gentleman. Yet he had a stilted air about him, an upright sort of stiffness that gave him the look of a mannequin in a shopwindow. It was as though he were not quite real, not completely human.

"No, sir," she said. "My student days are long behind me."

"Then you are the proprietress of the conservatory?"

"Oh no, for all the gardening at Longley Park is administered by Mr. Hedgley."

The man's dark eyebrows lifted. "Then may I ask who gives you the authority to refuse my request?"

Though the question was placed with civility, Clemma read the tinge of disdain it contained. But she had a ready answer.

"I am Clementine Laird, sir. My sister, Mrs. Ivy Richmond, is mistress of Longley."

"And this relationship gives you leave to make decisions regarding its citrus fruits?"

She looked to see if he were joking, but she recognized no hint of levity in his eyes. "My sister and her husband are away in India," she said. "But . . . no . . . I am not exactly in charge of making decisions here, for that would fall to Mr. Thompson, the family's solicitor. Or perhaps Mr. Wiggins, the butler, is responsible . . . though more rightly it might be the housekeeper, Mrs. Gold, for she is . . ." She paused and frowned. "At any rate, you may not purchase fruit from the conservatory. I am sorry."

Ducking behind her easel, she focused on her sketch of the vase as she hoped mightily that the man would go away. Instead, she heard again the sound of his footsteps approaching. Fearful lest he might peek at her drawing—which suddenly seemed poorly done indeed—Clemma rounded the easel and faced him.

"Sir, may I be so bold as to know your name?" she said. "I believe I may be compelled to report this incident of trespassing to the constable in Otley."

To her surprise, the man paled and took a step backward. "I beg you, do no such thing, Miss Laird. I come with no ill intent."

"Then who are you, and why must you continue to insist upon purchasing lemons and oranges?"

"I am a physician." He hesitated a moment. "My name is Paul Baine."

As he spoke those words, Clemma felt her blood plummet to her knees. "Dr. Baine?" she repeated numbly.

"Is my name familiar to you?"

"It most certainly is, sir." Trying to regain her composure, Clemma extended the stick of charcoal toward him, as if it were a sword that might protect her. From the earliest days of her youth, she had heard tales of the man who lived at Nasmyth Manor, the darkly shuttered house on a windswept fell some distance from the village of Otley. Dr. Baine kept himself and his practices hidden away—and it was well he did so, for had he flaunted his evils, the town would have driven him off.

It was rumored that women burdened with unwanted pregnancies slipped through the mists of night to knock on the door of Nasmyth Manor. In a day or two, they returned to their cottages, and not a word was spoken of what had taken place at the hands of Dr. Baine.

Not only did the man perform these unspeakable acts, but he also saw patients who had contracted diseases from their profligate activities. It was rumored that sailors came from Scarborough Harbour and the coastal cities of Hull, Whitby, and Filey to be treated with a special cure that Dr. Baine had developed. The fallen women who consorted with these men came, too, as did villagers who had ventured to Leeds for an evening of revelry and had returned with more than they had bargained for. The man who stood before Clemma had enriched himself by these most repulsive means. He was a fiend.

"Begone!" she cried, thrusting the charcoal stick at him. "Begone from this place, or I shall . . . I shall . . ."

"You need not fear me, Miss Laird—"

"I do not fear you—I revile you! Go away from here at once. As a Christian, I find that the very sight of you sickens me!"

A strange light flickered in his eyes. "You are a Christian. Of course." He shrugged his shoulders. "Nevertheless, I must have the citrus fruits, madam."

"Never. I would not allow you the smallest crumb from my table, let alone permit you to feast upon these beautiful oranges from my sister's hall."

"I do not want them for myself."

"No? And why should I believe anything you say?"

"Why should I believe anything *you* say? We are strangers, are we not? What you appear to know of me is only by rumor and reputation. I know you only by what you have chosen to reveal about yourself, Miss Laird."

"*Mrs.* Laird, if you please. I am a widow. And if you question my truthfulness, I shall . . . I shall . . ."

"You are not very good at making threats, Mrs. Laird," he said, one corner of his elegant mouth tipping up. "Madam, I have very politely approached you and begged permission to purchase fruit. It is not to be eaten by me, whom you seem to find so odious, but by someone who is in dire need of the sustenance it provides. And so I implore you, Mrs. Laird. I appeal to your Christian charity. May you please find it in your pious and devoted heart to assist one so far beneath you as my humble self?"

So saying, he fell on one knee, his arms outstretched and his head bowed.

Clemma was so stunned she hardly knew what to say. There could be no denying the depths of Dr. Baine's wickedness. Though she had never met him before, the tales of his villainous treatments had persisted so many years that they could not be anything but true. He rarely came into the village, and he never set foot in church. If he had, he would have been shunned by one and all.

Yet, this vile man had pointed out Clemma's Christian duty to act charitably. How could she refuse the fruit to one who must be in great need of its nourishment? But what if Dr. Baine planned to eat the oranges and lemons himself? What if his story were all a lie? Then she would be playing directly into his hand.

"Get up at once, sir," she said, irritated at the

indecision that plagued her. Did a Christian have an obligation to help those less fortunate—no matter what? No matter if the one in need was some bedraggled creature who had chosen to end the precious life growing within her womb? No matter if the hungry soul was a pestilent seaman who had spread his filth from port to port around the world? Oh, dear!

"Sir, I beg you to rise," she said again. "Your mockery disgusts me, and your posturing is insufferable."

"I shall rise only when you have permitted me to purchase oranges and lemons," he said, his head still bowed. "I cannot leave this place without accomplishing my mission."

Clemma stared down at the man's bent head. His dark hair was in need of a trim, but the collar of his white shirt had been crisply starched and pressed. The fabric was very fine, she noted, and the cut of his frock coat bespoke exquisite tailoring. No doubt his coffers had been well filled by those wretched and desperate souls who came to him in their need. Of course he could charge any price for his services, for no respectable physician would undertake such unmentionable tasks. Indeed, the practice was illegal, Clemma felt sure, though no one who had made use of it would dare to testify against him. Certainly Dr. Baine was the only such doctor in this entire region of Yorkshire, and his wealth must be immeasurable.

"Five pounds," she said. "Per orange."

His head shot up. "Five pounds for a single orange? You must be mad!"

"I am not. You can afford to pay my price, and as I possess the only oranges in Yorkshire on this particular November day, you have no choice. Agree to it now, or I shall raise the price to seven pounds."

"Preposterous!" he said, rising.

"No more so than the outrageous fees you surely must charge for your despicable practices. Five pounds per orange. And I shall place your money into the offering box at church, where it may be washed clean and then put to good use ministering to the needy in the name of Jesus Christ."

The icy blue eyes narrowed. "Mrs. Laird," he snarled, "you are not a godly woman."

"Oh, yes I am!" she cried, stepping toward him. "I worship Jesus as Lord and Savior, I go to church every Sunday, I do good deeds for the poor, and I do *not* associate with wicked men such as yourself!"

"Five pounds, then," he said, jerking his wallet from his coat. "Fetch me an orange!"

Clemma grabbed the money he held out and set off down the path toward the orangery. Such a horrid man! He did not deserve anything good in this life. She had half a mind to throw his money back at him and run outside to call for assistance in ridding Longley Park of such a miscreant.

But in the years since her husband's death, Clemma had learned to rely on no one but God and herself. She could certainly handle Dr. Baine without any help. Eyeing the double rows of healthy trees, she selected a small, greenish fruit and plucked it from the limb. There, that sour thing would do him very well.

When she swung around, she realized he stood directly behind her on the path. "Your orange, Dr. Baine," she said, handing it to him.

"I need another." He held out a second five-pound note. "I must have it. And how much will you charge me for a lemon?"

Clemma was about to send him away with another harsh rebuke when she recognized something in his face that startled her. He was pleading. His eyes were filled with a mixture of hope and doubt, and the set of his jaw revealed the utmost solemnity. At that moment Clemma saw the truth: He did *need* the oranges. He needed them desperately. He would pay her outrageous prices without further complaint.

"For whom do you seek these oranges?" she asked.

He gazed down at the pathetic little fruit in his hand. "For one who must have them." Pausing a moment, he added, "I cannot say more."

Without hesitation, Clemma reached up and tugged two more oranges from the tree. Then she hurried to the edge of the small grove and pulled down a handful of lemons. "Here, take these, sir, and begone." She thrust them into his hands. "And do not come to this place again, I beg you."

"You will not take payment for the remainder of the fruit, Mrs. Laird?"

"I do not want it."

"You are good."

She lifted her head. "A moment ago you doubted my Christianity. Am I now different?"

"Perhaps. I believe all humans to be capable of change for the better. Your behavior toward me has demonstrated the validity of this notion. I am grateful." He gave her a small bow. "And now I see that your tea has arrived. I do hope the milk is warm. Good day, Mrs. Laird."

Clemma stared after him as he hurried away down the path. He passed the footman who bore a tray of tea things, and then he slipped through the glass door and was gone. Clemma started toward her easel, but the image of asters had been replaced in her thoughts by the memory of a pair of strangely beckoning blue eyes.

⊠ ⊠ ⊠

Paul Baine turned the iron skeleton key in the lock and pushed open the large wooden doors of

Nasmyth Manor. Fear of reprisals from the towns-
folk had driven away most of the family servants
years before, and so he walked alone to the
mirrored coatrack and hung up his top hat and
cloak. Moments before, he had stabled and fed his
horse, and soon he would journey down to the
kitchen to make a little supper.

But now he stood in front of the large dusty
mirror and gazed at the man reflected in the cold
glass. When had so many threads of his hair turned to
silver? When had his skin become lined with traces of
age? What had become of the little boy who once ran
up and down the moorlands, skinning his knees,
playing in brooks, and climbing to the top of the
mount known as the Chevin? Where was the youth
who had traveled away to London to learn the practice of medicine? Full of idealism, a young Paul
Baine had dreamed of returning to his home and
family, marrying a lovely woman, and filling a
bustling office with his patients.

But both his parents had died while he was away
at school, too soon to see their son fulfill his
dreams—and thankfully too soon to know the depths
of degradation into which he would fall. He had
never married. And the busy medical practice had
become nothing more than a castle in the clouds.
Instead, frightened men and women crept up to his
doors at night, filled with fear of Nasmyth Manor

and contempt for its owner—yet too needy to shun his services.

Oh, he was wealthy enough. Yet what good had all his money ever done him? Until now, none. But some months ago, a faint flicker of possibility had come to life inside his heart. The vague idea had given him hope. As it took shape, it had led him to step out, to act boldly, to do what he never thought he could do. And now . . . most unexpectedly . . . he had found reason to live.

Turning away from the mirror, Paul hurried down a marbled corridor and pushed aside a heavy curtain of green baize. He would not allow himself to think of the tart-tongued Mrs. Laird, whose sparkling eyes and pink cheeks had both surprised and entranced him. How long had it been since he'd seen a woman in the prime of health, a woman glorying in the sunshine that lit up her pale blonde curls? How long since he had engaged in an actual conversation with a lovely creature of intelligence and education? How long since he had felt even slightly human?

With a shake of his head, he dismissed the ache in his heart and hurried down a long flight of steps into the frigid kitchen. With the aged cook already gone for the day, the fire had died out as usual. Suddenly weary, Paul sighed and laid kindling on the hearth. The sulfurous smell of the match striking the brick and igniting brought him awake again. He must see to the tasks ahead.

Moving quickly, he located a juicer in the pantry and reamed the three oranges until their pulp was dry. Then he laid a few logs on the fire, poured the juice into a small pitcher, and started back up the stairs.

Clementine Laird was lovely and bright, he reflected as he made his way down the unlit hallways of the east wing, but she was far more acidic than any lemon. She held herself in high regard and occupied her time with nothing more useful than painting flowers. Though she claimed to be a Christian, her heart had grown hard and proud. No, indeed, Paul decided as he pushed through a door at the far end of the corridor. He would think no more of the vain woman.

"Alice?" he whispered. "Are you awake?"

"Aye, Dr. Baine. I canna sleep, sir. Me joints is achin'."

He approached the bed on which the poor woman lay. Instantly, the foul odor of her illness overwhelmed him, and it was a moment before he could bring himself to be seated on the stool nearby. In the waning light, he drew back the sheet that covered her and studied the worsening effects of the disease.

"I lost three more teeth while ye were out, Dr.

Baine," Alice said, pointing to the table where they lay. "If I live, I'll never be able to eat meat again."

As a tear ran down her pale cheek, he parted her lips and examined her diseased gums. "Ah, now, Alice, enough of that talk. You will live, and you will eat all the meat your heart desires—provided you mash it a bit first. Perhaps we shall even find you a denture in the market."

"Ah, Dr. Baine, ye know I canna pay for such a thing!"

"I shall buy it for you then."

"Ye be too good to me, sir!" Her worn hand reached out to stroke his cheek as he carefully examined the blackened lesions in her armpits and the enlargement of her joints.

"Do you feel movement today, Alice?" he asked carefully.

"Aye, sir." She began to weep again. "But not much."

Worried about the unborn child that swelled the woman's belly . . . *his* unborn son or daughter . . . he placed his hands on her skin until he, too, felt the slightest motion beneath them. "The baby lives, and you must live." He took the pitcher of juice and poured the orange liquid into a glass. "Now then, Alice, you must drink this."

"I canna drink, Dr. Baine! Me mouth 'urts too much. Me teeth is all out, and me jaws is—"

"Drink, Alice. If you wish to become well, you must drink this juice. All of it."

Despite the foul odor, he slipped his arm behind her neck and lifted her head until he was able to pour the juice into her bloodied mouth. At first, she gagged. But as the nourishing tonic began to fill her stomach, she clutched at the glass and drank and drank until not a drop remained.

"Better?" he asked as she dropped back onto the pillow.

"Ah, sir, ye have brought me 'eaven itself! Oh, God be praised! Have ye more? Dr. Baine, I feel I could drink that juice until I float away on a river of 'appiness!"

Paul reflected on the pert Clementine Laird and her parting words: *"Do not come to this place again."* The thought of facing her accusations and rebukes turned inside him like a knife. He was well acquainted with such sanctimonious souls. It was people like Mrs. Laird who kept him from the streets and shops of Otley, and it was their ridicule and ostracism that kept him from their social gatherings, their town meetings, and their church.

"I have a few lemons," he said, draping the damp sheet over Alice's ravaged body. "You will have sweet lemon juice at ten o'clock tonight. And then, you must try to sleep."

"But after t' lemons is gone, sir? Can ye fetch me more of them oranges? Please, sir!"

"It is difficult, Alice. I do not go out among people easily."

"Ye dread what they'll say about ye, eh?" She laid her hand on his. "'Twas such thinkin' as drove me 'ere, Dr. Baine, to Nasmyth Manor. I could not bear what folks might say about me in t' village. Me parents would've tossed me out of t' cottage. But ye gave me courage. Ye showed me 'ow to do t' right thing. Now ye must 'ave courage yerself."

Paul squeezed Alice's frail fingers. "We shall see," he said, standing. "And now you should rest."

As he walked to the door, he heard her call out behind him, "Dr. Baine!"

"Yes, Alice?"

"God will give ye t' courage," she said. "Pray, sir. Pray for courage!"

Paul studied the draped figure and then pulled the door to. Because of Alice, he thought, perhaps now God would hear his prayers.

TWO

Only two days had passed since Alice had swallowed the first sips of orange juice, but her recovery was marked. Her eyes had brightened, the ache in her joints had eased, and her gums had ceased to bleed. Paul Baine was highly pleased.

Yet, as he stood gazing down at his sleeping patient, he realized how temporary the changes could be. Alice must have more oranges. The child inside her lived and was nearly ready to be born. If the woman were to successfully deliver a healthy infant and nurse it through its first months of life, she must recover from this deadly scourge. The thought of the baby's birth sent a prickle of anticipation down his spine. A baby . . . *his* baby . . .

But to get the fruit, he must encounter that snippy Clementine Laird again—not a pleasant prospect in the least. Perhaps she would not be in the conservatory this day, he mused. Perhaps one of the gardeners could be persuaded to part with the oranges more readily. If Paul could come away with a large bag of fruit, he would not need to return there in the near future.

There was no option in the matter, he decided finally. He must go back to Longley Park, and he must depart at once.

Without allowing himself to debate the issue further, he left Alice's room and made his way to the foyer. There, he donned his warm black wool cloak and top hat, wrapped a scarf around his throat, and stepped outside into the biting wind. In minutes, he had saddled his horse and was riding down the road toward the grand estate belonging to the Richmond family.

Mrs. Laird was well connected, for the Richmonds had built a vast fortune in India. Her sister must be pleased with the match she had made—or perhaps their fathers had arranged the marriage. At one time, Paul had considered speaking to his solicitor in London about the possibility of making such a connection for himself. But the thought of bringing any wife into the hostile environment of Otley village and its environs had quickly stifled his desires. Not even the high walls and numerous rooms of Nasmyth Manor could protect a woman from the derision and hatred that would come with being the wife of *that man.* That awful Dr. Baine. No woman would consider marrying him. He understood that now. He had accepted his fate.

As he rode through the massive iron gates of Longley Park, Paul again squelched the ache of loneliness that twisted inside his chest. He had made his choices. He had followed a path of his own creation. Nothing could change that.

As he reined his horse, he spotted an old fellow stacking clay pots just outside the soaring glass walls of the conservatory. "Good morning to you, my good man," he called.

"Eh? Oh, I dinna hear ye, sir." Straightening, he tipped his ragged felt hat. "T' name is 'edgley, and I be t' 'ead gardener round these parts. 'ow may I be of service?"

"The head gardener? Wonderful!" Paul swung down from his horse and approached the fellow. "I came here two days ago and purchased several citrus fruits for a patient in my care. I wonder if you might be so kind as to fill this sack with oranges, lemons, and limes. I shall pay you handsomely."

Hedgley peered at the large woven bag and scratched the side of his head. "'em oranges is fer t' art students wot take residence at t' great 'ouse. We canna sell 'em to t' public."

"I understand, but this is a special case, my good man. They are needed most urgently."

"Ye be a doctor?" He tipped his head, squinting into the morning sun. "I never saw ye before, sir."

"That is because . . . because I am a doctor who . . . I am Dr. Paul Baine, and the young lady allowed me—"

"Dr. Baine?" The rheumy blue eyes widened, and the kindly expression transformed into one of horror and disgust. "Dr. Baine wot lives over at Nasmyth Manor . . . ye be 'im?"

"Look, it hardly matters who I am. The point is, Mrs. Laird saw fit to provide me the fruit."

"She did, did she?"

"Indeed. And now I am here to purchase more."

"Then be my guest. T' good lady paints 'er flowers inside as usual. Go in and beg yer boon of 'er."

"No, please, I do not wish to—"

"Good day, sir. I must be off." He tipped his hat again. "Work calls me, ye understand."

Casting a wary backward glance, Hedgley toddled off as fast as his swayed back and knobby knees would take him. As if fleeing from a ghost, Paul thought. And now he must again face Mrs. Laird.

Pushing open the conservatory door, he stepped inside and took a deep breath of the steamy air. The glass walls rose toward the blue November sky, a crystalline arch that welcomed the sun yet barred any hint of chill. Inside, hundreds of green and growing things pushed upward toward the light. Ferns, philodendrons, palms, and fruit trees mingled with flowering camellias, fragrant gardenias, and cascades of pink, yellow, and red roses. The place was a feast for the senses—all color and warmth and vibrant life.

Encouraged, Paul stepped onto one of the sandy paths that had been laid out inside the conservatory. He removed his hat and draped his cloak over his arm as he strolled past a patch of potted Asiatic lilies. They bowed to a tall banana tree hung with ripe golden fruit. Princesses in bright saris fawning over a grand maharaja. Smiling at the image, he rounded a cluster of tall forsythia bushes . . . and there she stood.

Mrs. Clementine Laird hovered over a small clay pot, her fingers poking down into the lush growth of a green plant. Her pretty pink mouth was drawn into a pout, and a smudge of dirt marred the porcelain sheen of her cheek. Clearly dissatisfied with her examination, she set her hands on her hips, leaned forward, and loudly commanded, *"Bloom!"*

Caught off guard, Paul nearly laughed aloud. Catching himself just in time, he took a deep breath and was about to address her, when—

"Bloom, you naughty hellebore!" she cried. "Do you hear me? I have done everything I know to do for you. You've had a lovely meal of fresh compost and a long drink of water every day. What more can you possibly want?"

She gave the pot a half turn. "There. Is that better?" She tilted her head and gazed at the plant.

For a moment, Paul could neither move nor speak. Bonnetless, her hair had been swept high onto her head, a gleaming bounty of golden glory. Long dark lashes framed eyes the brilliant blue of a Yorkshire summer sky. A pale blue gown, modestly buttoned, covered her slender form. She could not, however, hide the sight of her ivory neck. The unexpected longing Paul felt at this vision of loveliness gave him away. He must have emitted some audible sound, for her head shot up and she gasped in dismay.

"Oh, my goodness gracious!"

"I am terribly sorry," he said, stepping forward, fearful lest she faint of shock. "I did not mean to startle you."

"Wretched man! How long have you been standing there?"

"Only a moment. Please, do calm yourself."

"One should announce one's presence, Dr. Baine," she said, taking up a scrap of sketch paper and fanning herself. "It is terribly rude to do otherwise."

"Indeed it is. Please accept my apologies." He hardly knew what to say next, for her cheeks had grown bright pink and the sketch paper trembled in her hand. "I fear I have greatly unsettled you."

"You have . . . and I . . . did you hear . . . was I . . ."

"You were admonishing the hellebore, but—"

"Oh, dear! I beg you to leave my presence at once, sir. Your company is not welcome here."

"I assure you, I often speak to plants myself, Mrs. Laird," he continued, electing to ignore her hostility. "I have a large hothouse on my property, and I take much delight in experimenting with the propagation of herbs and flowers. I am particularly taken with roses, which often misbehave and must be reproved on a regular basis for their stubbornness."

At this, her lips parted and a soft smile stole across them. "You reprove your roses?"

"When they are naughty. But when they do well, of course, I congratulate them heartily and give them an extra large helping of compost."

"Oh." She held the sketch paper over her mouth, but he could hear the small giggle that escaped her lips. "I am quite sure the gardeners here at Longley would not approve of your technique."

"Perhaps not, but I would challenge any of them to reproduce this particular dashing yellow rose with its fragrance a mixture of lemon and spice. A more manly specimen has never been seen."

"I confess, I have never seen a manly flower in my life."

"This one is a fine specimen of masculinity. Handsome indeed, and most well behaved."

"I see." She was smiling now, and skepticism gave way to a sparkle of merriment in her blue eyes. "How fascinating."

"And what seems to be the trouble with your hellebore?"

"It will not bloom, though I brought it inside many weeks ago and have coddled it with great tenderness."

"Perhaps it needs a bit stronger discipline. Allow me." He picked up the pot and glared at the small green plant. "Now see here, young lady. A bloom is required of you, and I command you to produce one. Or else!"

He set the pot back onto the table. "There, Mrs. Laird. I believe you shall have satisfaction soon."

Blushing, she dipped him a small curtsy. "I would be grateful for that."

"And I am pleased to be of service. May I also inform you that the oranges and lemons you so graciously provided on our last meeting have had a most salutary effect."

Her smile faded. "I am glad to hear it."

"Unfortunately, more citrus fruit is required. My patient cannot fully recover without it."

Somber now, she glanced at her easel as if eager to return to her painting and to be done with him. "I spoke with Mrs. Winchell, the head cook at the great house, Dr. Baine. She needs the oranges for the art students. I am sorry."

His fear for his patient's welfare manifested itself in a wave of irritation, and he forced down the harsh words that formed on his tongue. "Mrs. Laird, these fruits are for a very ill patient. How can you refuse to sell them to me?"

"Do not trifle with my intelligence, sir. What sort of illness can possibly be cured by oranges?"

"Scurvy, of course!" He regretted his tone instantly, for her face paled and she shrank into herself.

"I did not know that."

"A physician named James Lind proposed it as a cure in the last century. It was tested and proven to be effective, though no one is able to ascertain why. For the past fifty years, Mrs. Laird, the Royal Navy has provided a daily ration of lime or lemon juice to its sailors while at sea."

"I am sorry," she mumbled. "I am not familiar with the practices of our navy. Then . . . then your patient is a seaman?"

He could see the more significant question behind her query. If the patient were a sailor, she would reason, he must have come to Dr. Baine for treatment of another lethal illness. Venereal diseases plagued the men of the Royal Navy, and the growth of the British Empire meant the ravages of those virulent plagues had spread to native women around the globe. No cures had been discovered, though treatments could be taken to ease the symptoms. Paul Baine himself had developed such a tonic, for he grew more than roses in his hothouse.

"You would object to my treating a sailor with scurvy?" he asked.

She shrugged. "Why should he come to you if rations of lemon juice are to be had on board his ship?"

"Why indeed?"

"Perhaps he came to you for . . . for another reason?"

"A venereal disease, you mean?"

"Goodness!" Her cheeks instantly suffused a bright scarlet. "I did not say *that!*"

"No, but you meant it. I ask you, Mrs. Laird. Is one disease less worthy of treatment by a physician than another? Is an illness that arises from a lack of citrus fruits somehow more worthy than one that is transmitted through sexual misconduct?"

"Sin, you mean."

"Of course." Frankly, he was surprised she had not fainted dead away by this time. Such bold discussion of delicate matters was hardly the realm of sensitive young ladies. Yet, Clementine Laird seemed quite willing to engage in debate.

"Sin must always be reproved, Dr. Baine. One must never condone behavior that defies the express commands of God."

"Does healing the human body defy any holy command?"

"I do not believe the Bible speaks to the matter of healing those with such . . . such wicked diseases. Diseases that are the consequence of sin."

He mused on this for a moment. "May I ask you a question, Mrs. Laird?"

She glanced at her easel again, but he sensed she was as willing to continue their discussion as he. "I suppose so."

"Which is of greater consequence to God—the human body or the soul?"

"The soul, of course."

"And did not this Jesus Christ whom you worship redeem the souls of those who had committed sin? If I recall from my childhood lessons in church, he befriended a cheating tax collector and forgave a woman living with a man who was not her husband. I believe he even refused to condemn someone caught in the act of adultery. I ask you then, Mrs. Laird, if God were willing to heal the souls of such reprehensible creatures, would he object to a physician who attempts to cure their earthly bodies?"

She thought about this for a moment, one finger turning a loose curl that had slipped from the bun at the back of her head. "I suppose not," she said finally, "though I cannot understand why a highly trained physician should stoop to such depths."

"Perhaps because he cares about those whom others have rejected. Perhaps he sees the utter hopelessness of a life blighted by prejudicial hatred. Perhaps he understands what it is to be reviled and ridiculed and cast off by polite society."

She swallowed as her large blue eyes filled with sudden tears. "I suppose there is reason to assist such wretched people."

"Sin comes in many forms, Mrs. Laird."

Nodding, she attempted to blink away the tears. "Indeed it does, and an unloving heart is among the worst of sins. Is your poor sailor quite incapacitated by the scurvy?"

"My patient is not a sailor but a young woman. She came to see me about . . . about another matter, and upon examining her, I recognized the symptoms of scurvy. My usual source for citrus fruits was unable to supply them this late in the year. The patient's condition worsened almost to the point of death. It was nearly too late to save her life when I remembered the conservatory at Longley Park."

"Come to the orangery, sir," Clementine said at once. "You must take as many oranges and lemons as you like. I believe we even have a lime tree or two."

Beckoning him, she whirled away from her easel and hurried ahead down a path toward the small grove of potted trees. As the hooped and crinolined bell of her skirt swung from side to side, Paul found himself thinking how wonderful it would be to spend hours in the company of the lovely Clementine Laird. Her tongue might be sharp, but her heart was soft. Moreover, she had a quick intelligence and an easy smile, and he found her intriguing.

"Oh no!" she cried, turning so quickly that the hem of her skirt swirled around and rose to reveal a pair of lovely silk slippers and a most enchanting pair of ankles. Paul could hardly keep his eyes from them, but her distress drew his attention.

"Someone has taken all the ripe oranges!" she said. "These are small and green, and they will never do for juice. Now that I think upon the matter, I recall Mrs. Winchell saying yesterday that she intended to make baked orange puddings for the art students today, and that means she must use both the rinds and the juice! She has clearly ordered all the ripe oranges plucked and brought to the house. By this time of day, she will have baked the puddings, and it will be too late!"

Dismayed, he scanned the double rows of trees and discovered that she was absolutely correct. There was not a single ripe orange.

"Perhaps there are still lemons." She lifted her skirt and raced to the end of the grove. "Yes! Yes, Dr. Baine, you shall have lemons. I see several that look very good. Here is one! And another!"

Together they managed to find a dozen lemons of sufficient ripeness. Paul slipped them into his bag along with a handful of limes and a single orange that somehow had been missed. It would be enough to sustain Alice's recovery for a short time.

"May I come again?" he asked as they walked together toward the conservatory door. "I believe these will last four or five days at the most."

"Indeed, you must come back," she said. "And in the meantime, I shall examine the trees every day and set aside for you any oranges that ripen."

"Will you be here when I return?" He knew the question could be seen as a practical matter. But the flush of color to her cheeks and her shy glance away told him she understood its true meaning.

"I come to the conservatory to paint every day but Sunday," she said softly.

"Then I shall be sure to stay away on that day. And now may I ask the sum I am to pay for these fruits?"

She hesitated a moment. "This woman—is she your . . . your wife?"

"No, Mrs. Laird. I have never married."

"Ah." She let out a breath and managed a little nod. "But of course there is no charge for the fruit, and I am remorseful for taking your five pounds. No, the fruit goes to a charitable cause, and you must have it without cost."

Paul thought about the pouch of coins he had brought from Nasmyth Manor, a substantial sum. "Did you give my five pounds to the church?" he asked.

"I took it there on my way home that very day."

"Will you take this as well?" He drew the heavy pouch from his coat and held it out to her.

"My goodness, sir, this is a great deal of money! Surely you did not bring all of this to pay for oranges?"

"I did, and now I shall send the money away to church to pay for other things."

"To pay for what?"

"God requires such recompense of us, does he not, along with good deeds and moral behavior? Therefore, take it, Mrs. Laird, and give it to God."

Not wishing to explain his actions further, he bowed, tossed his cloak around his shoulders, and stepped out into the crisp winter day.

"Mama, I have a question of great moral import,"
Clementine began as the maid cleared away the
breakfast dishes. At Brooking House, discussions
of social and doctrinal matters had always been
encouraged. Indeed, when all the family were
assembled during Clemma's childhood, mealtimes
had often gone on for hours—especially when Papa
began to recite lengthy passages from the Bible or
from one of his favorite poems.

"Is it right," she asked, "for a physician to treat
unmentionable diseases which have been contracted
by the most reprehensible elements of society?"

"Goodness, Clemma! Such a question to ask at
the dining table." Mrs. Bowden blotted her lips
with a napkin. "Let us discuss your November
painting instead. Is it turning out to be as lovely as
I predicted? And what of your stubborn flower?
That . . . that *helle*-whatever?"

"Hellebore. Papa, what do you think of my
question? Should intelligent, moral doctors treat
wicked people who are ill because of their own sin?"

"A very good question, my dear girl," Papa
replied, leaning back in his chair. "Sin has many
earthly consequences, not the least of which is
disease. Ministers are called upon to tend to the
souls of the blackest of sinners. And I suppose godly

physicians must tend the bodies of these same transgressors."

"Oh, I cannot think this is true, dearest," Mama said. "One should shun such offenders. Good society must not be polluted by contact with those who have not our grace, our education, our fine manners. Giving charity is one thing. We must take baskets of food to the hungry cottagers, send tonics to the ill, and give our money to the church for its ongoing ministries. But stepping into the midst of those who practice sin—and thereby appearing to condone their behaviors—should never be undertaken. It is a grave mistake."

Clemma studied her mother, still lovely even into the years of her advancing age. Though her golden hair had faded almost to white, her plump, pink cheeks and sparkling blue eyes were a testament to good health. The years had been less kind to Papa, whose knees were stricken with painful gout and who had, unfortunately, lost most of his hair and teeth.

"Now, now, Mrs. Bowden," he said, "one must always look to the example of Christ. He did not hesitate to step into the midst of sinners."

"But *we* are not to do such a thing, Mr. Bowden! Can you imagine a world in which young ladies educated in the very finest arts—embroidery, beading, flower arranging, and painting, as is our dearest Clemma—would leave their parlors and drawing rooms to mingle among wicked, diseased people who live in hovels? I can hardly think of it without becoming faint."

"Now then, calm yourself, my dear," Papa interjected.

"A good physician," she went on, "a well-trained and highly educated man of medicine, should tend to the ill of his own society. We have our dreadful diseases, have we not? Gout and consumption and the like—not to mention those of us ladies with delicate nerves! Let the people of the lower classes be tended by their own kind. The shops are full of tonics enough to ease their pain. I am not without sympathy for those sorts of people, but goodness gracious, it is unthinkable that an upstanding, well-mannered gentleman like this doctor Clemma has met, this . . . this . . . what is the young man's name, by the way?"

So surprised was Clemma by the sudden question that she inhaled a sip of tea. Coughing, she thought this might make a good excuse for a hasty exit from the dining room and the uncomfortable turn of the conversation. But her throat cleared too quickly, and she was left gazing into the kind blue eyes of her mother.

"It was just a question, really, Mama," she said.

"No, but you must have someone in mind. Have

you met some fine young doctor in the village? Or is this physician finding time in his schedule to paint with the other artists at Longley Park? Perhaps you became acquainted in the conservatory?"

"Oh, Mama, please—"

"I can see by the blush of your cheeks that I have guessed rightly. Please, my darling girl, do tell us about your gentleman friend."

"Yes, yes," Papa said, "your mother will winkle it out of you one way or another. Come along, then. Tell us all about the fellow."

Clemma clenched her napkin, searching wildly for some honest yet indirect response to their request. If they knew she had met the infamous Dr. Baine of Nasmyth Manor, Mama would probably faint dead away. Papa would forbid Clemma to go near the conservatory again. Though she was a grown woman and had been their caretaker for many years, they continued to see her as their youngest daughter, the baby of the family.

"Well," she began, "I did meet someone—"

"There! I knew it!" Mama clapped her hands in delight. "And a doctor! Dear Mr. Bowden, is this not a happy piece of news? Are you not delighted?"

"Mama, please do not mistake the relationship. He is much older than I . . . I think . . . and we merely engaged in a philosophical discussion about—"

"Is he handsome?" Mama cried.

"Yes, but—"

"Oh, I do hope he does not carry you away to London or Plymouth or some other foreign place! Tell me he lives nearby, my dear, for I cannot bear to see you taken from us."

"He lives near Otley."

"Marvelous!"

"But here is the greater question," Papa said. "Now that he has moved into Yorkshire, does he mean to take on patients from the lower classes? Those with unmentionable diseases? Those who cannot afford to pay well?"

"Well, he does treat such people—"

"I should advise him against it immediately, my dear. If he means to keep you in the proper society, he must have the money and the connections to do so. As Homer so wisely put it, 'There is nothing greater and better than this—when a husband and wife keep a household in oneness of mind, a great woe to their enemies and joy to their friends, and win high renown.' It is all well and good to have charitable intentions toward the poor, but one must be practical when taking a wife."

"Papa, please! This man has no interest in taking me as his wife."

"Is he already married?" Mama asked, her blue eyes suddenly filled with trepidation.

"No, he has never married, and he certainly does not intend to marry me!"

"Aha! I thought as much! Did I not tell you, Mr. Bowden, that our darling daughter would marry again? I knew it would happen. And a doctor! Oh, you will be given the greatest respect when we all go into town or attend a ball."

"Mama, please!" Clemma cried, the lump in her throat growing painfully large. "Mama, he does not mean to marry me, nor I him!"

"But why ever not?" As she spoke the words, recognition dawned on her face. "Have you told him about . . . does he know . . . have you mentioned . . . ?"

"No, Mama, he does not know anything about my past, and I shall never tell him about the . . . the situation." Tears suddenly sprang into her eyes, and she pushed away from the table. "I must go now. Do excuse me."

"Oh, darling, I am sure he would understand! He loves you very much indeed."

"Mama, he does not love me! We have barely met."

"But you love him! I can see it in your eyes when you speak of him. Please, dear Clemma, do not shut him out of your heart. I am sure he will love you no matter what has happened . . . no matter that you are . . . that the matter exists."

Brushing a tear from her cheek, Clemma gazed at her adoring, well-meaning parents. How desperately she longed to please them. But marriage could never be.

"He will not marry me, Mama," she said softly. "No man will. I shall never allow it."

Before they could answer, she ran from the room. Gathering up her box of paints and brushes, she tried to turn her thoughts to her paintings and the exhibition that would celebrate her work. She pulled on a coat, set a plain bonnet on her head, and tied the ribbon at her throat. The conservatory beckoned with its promise of warmth and light and vibrant life. Perhaps she would finish painting the asters today, and perhaps there would be more ripe oranges on the trees, and perhaps . . . perhaps *he* would come again.

THREE

"Michaelmas daisies is wot ye got there," Mr. Hedgley said. "I'd know 'em anywhere."

"Indeed, but they are properly known as asters." Clemma leaned forward and brushed a dab of yellow in the center of one of the small purple flowers on her easel. "Aster is the scientific name, you see."

"Wot ye be wantin' to give it a scientific name fer? Michaelmas daisy suits it just fine."

"I am not responsible for the name, Mr. Hedgley. A botanist must have designated the flower as an aster."

"Botanist." The old man snorted. "I wager I could get more Michaelmas daisies to grow than any 'botanist.' A gardener is wot ye want if ye mean to grow flowers. Not a book-ridden scientist."

"Science can be a good thing. I was speaking to . . . to someone just the other day about the cultivation and breeding of roses. And he said—"

"It were 'im, weren't it? That Dr. Baine. I seen 'im go into t' conservatory. 'e told me ye gives 'im oranges and such."

"He has a patient who needs citrus fruit. She suffers from scurvy." Clemma set her brush on the table, for her hand had suddenly begun to tremble. "Mr. Hedgley, I beg you, please do not tell anyone about Dr. Baine coming here."

"It ain't seemly, ye talkin' to a chap like that. Ye a fine lady, and 'im? He's a rotter. Not worthy to be looked upon by t' likes of ye."

"It is quite possible that his reputation is undeserved. He does seem to be—"

"Nay! Wot they tell about 'im is true, Mrs. Laird. I knows it. Some fifteen years ago, more or less, me granddaughter got 'erself into trouble, she did, and afore we could think wot to do, off she went to Nasmyth Manor. She come back 'ome two days later, and that were t' end of t' matter. An abomination, that man is. 'e don't deserve to breathe t' same air as a proper young lady like yerself."

Clemma found she could not remain standing at her easel. She had hoped—prayed!—that the stories about Dr. Baine might be proven false. He had been truly gentlemanlike with her, and he clearly cared about his patient.

"Are you quite sure it was Dr. Baine?" she asked the gardener.

"It were 'im, no doubt about it. 'e's a bad, bad man."

"But are we not all sinners, Mr. Hedgley? Your granddaughter, for example, committed a grave trespass in the eyes of God. Two, in fact. First she compromised herself without the benefit of wedlock, and then she elected to end the life of the child that was growing inside her. You have forgiven your granddaughter, sir, yet you classify Dr. Baine's sin as unforgivable. I believe that all of us, in one way or another—"

"Nay, lass, do not take that pathway! We be sinners, aye, but we don't make a practice of it. And when we sin, we goes straight to t' church and begs forgiveness of God. Me granddaughter got 'erself wedded to a fine farm boy, and now she 'as five strappin' young lads and two wee daughters to call 'er own. She mended 'er ways right off, see. But Dr. Baine lives a *life* of sin, 'e does. If ye ask me, that man be evil. Evil and wicked as t' devil hisself."

Clemma thought of the gentleman whose blue eyes had haunted her thoughts. She knew the devil could disguise himself as an angel of light. Deceit and lies were his primary tools. Could it be true that

Dr. Baine was an agent of Satan? Surely he must be if Mr. Hedgley spoke the truth! Oh, why had she given him the oranges? Why had she allowed herself to speak with him so freely and cordially?

"I believe you must be correct, Mr. Hedgley," she said, taking out a handkerchief and patting her temples. "If you know for a fact that he makes a practice of this . . . this abomination . . . then he can be nothing but a demon in Satan's army, and we should not ever speak—"

"Whisht!" The gardener reached out and set his fingers on her lips. "T' man hisself is 'ere! I seen 'im comin' through t' shrubberies just now. Shall I send 'im away?"

Clemma turned to see the tall figure moving down the path toward them. He looked haggard today, his hair atumble at the back of his neck, his frock coat unbuttoned. Spotting her, he lifted a hand, and his face brightened a little.

"No, Mr. Hedgley, I am not afraid of Dr. Baine," she said softly. "You may go on with your work."

"I'll not leave ye alone with 'im."

"You must. I shall be all right."

"Nay!"

"Mr. Hedgley, you are dismissed," she said firmly. Rising from the chair, she extended her hand. "Dr. Baine, you have come for the oranges."

He took her hand and bowed. "Mrs. Laird. You are looking well."

"Thank you. I have been painting since morning, and—" She glanced at the old gardener. "You may go now, Mr. Hedgley."

Muttering, he ambled away. She knew he would not wander far, and she was grateful for his concern. She turned back to the man who stood before her. "How is your patient?"

"Her health declines. I find I must visit her bedside every hour to assure myself that she lives."

"She stays at your house?"

"Certainly. I have devoted an entire wing of Nasmyth Manor to my infirmary."

"You have many patients then? But I thought . . ." An uncomfortable heat crept into her cheeks.

"What did you think, Mrs. Laird?"

She lifted her chin and met his eyes. "I supposed that you performed your . . . your surgeries . . . or dispensed your medicines and sent them on their way."

"Sometimes my patients choose to depart the house immediately. But quite often, they are unable or unwilling to go. And so I tend them in the infirmary. Some stay for many months."

"Months!"

"You do not suppose that all illnesses can be healed overnight, do you, Mrs. Laird? I am a good doctor, but I am not God."

"Certainly not, though I had imagined . . . I had believed that you, well, that . . . at any rate," she went on quickly, "I have set aside quite a number of oranges for your patient who suffers from scurvy. I pray they will not come too late."

"Alice and I are most grateful."

Alice. The sound of the woman's name skittered down Clemma's spine. This patient was a real person suddenly. A human being.

"You call her Alice?" she asked, surprised at the familiarity between doctor and patient.

"It is her name. She comes from Hull. I have not been treating her long, but I sense she is a good woman. I should be most unhappy were she to perish. It would mean a great deal to me, Mrs. Laird, if you would pray for her."

"I shall be glad to. Shall we both pray, you and I? That way Alice will stand a far greater chance of survival. For, as you know, the Bible clearly tells us that where two or three are gathered in God's name, there he is among them."

"I rarely address the Almighty. It is not my custom." He tipped his head. "And now may I collect the fruit and be on my way?"

For a moment, Clemma found herself immo-bile. A man who did not pray? But why? And then reality became clear. Naturally he would not pray. Such a sinner could never come before the throne of God in good conscience! Would God even listen to a man like Dr. Baine? Surely not.

"The oranges, Mrs. Laird?"

"Of course." She stepped behind her easel to the small table where she kept her palette, paints, charcoal sketching sticks, and the vase of fading asters. As she knelt to retrieve the basket she had used to collect the fruit, she pondered the matter of prayer once again.

If God refused to listen to the prayers of the wicked, then how might they ever come to him in confession and repentance? But if God did listen to sinners, then might it not be required of Christians to do likewise? For the Bible made it quite clear that Christians were to mold themselves into the image of Christ. If he loved and gave heed to the sinful, should not his disciples . . . should not Clemma herself . . . do the same?

Oh my, how distressing! she thought as she tugged the basket out from under the table. Was it possible that God had allowed the vile and reprehensible Dr. Baine into Clemma's life in order that she might lead him toward a heavenly path?

"Beautiful!" came the exclamation as she rose to her feet. "Dear lady, this is truly a magnificent work of art. I am all astonishment."

"But you were not to look! No one is to look!" Clemma cried, horrified to find that he had stepped around her easel and was gazing at her November painting. "It is not finished! I have a great deal more to do, and I am quite, quite displeased with the rose hips, for they are as flat as anything. And, dear me, I beg you to stop staring at it!"

"Certainly I am aware that this is a work in progress, Mrs. Laird. But do allow me to continue to study it, for I am rendered almost speechless by the detail and careful coloration with which you have brought these flowers to life upon the canvas."

"The rose hips, though, are clearly—"

"And this border of wheat sheaves has been created with such delicacy that the wheat appears almost to be waving in the breeze of an autumn day. Bravo!"

Stunned at his high praise, Clemma could do nothing but clasp the basket of oranges and gawk back and forth between her far-from-worthy painting and the man who was determined to admire it. He tilted his head one way. Then he took a step backward and turned his head the other way. Then he studied the bouquet of real flowers that was Clemma's model, the palette of watercolors used to paint the picture, and the array of brushes Clemma had employed. Finally, he took another step forward and observed the canvas again.

"The shading," he announced. "It is slightly amiss on the rose hips, I believe. Do you see how you have portrayed the light coming from this upper-left-hand direction and shining upon on the asters and the vase? Yet the rose hips do not show as great a reflection as they ought."

Clemma stepped up beside him and peered at her painting. "By george, you are quite right. No wonder they appear so flat."

"It should not take a great effort to correct the problem."

"No, not at all. I can right it immediately now that I know where I went wrong." Dipping her brush into the white paint, she mixed it with a little red and carefully began to highlight each berry. "A little more shading would help, do you not agree?"

"Indubitably."

She painted a little dark brown on the undersides of the rose hips, and suddenly they sprang off the canvas as if they were alive.

"*Voilà!*" Dr. Baine cried, throwing his arm around her shoulders and giving her a warm hug. "You have done it, Mrs. Laird! Congratulations!"

"But only with your help! I could not see what was wrong with them, and now it is so clear. Thank you very much indeed!" For an instant, she drifted into his embrace and laid her head on his shoulder. "A perfect solution, and now I can rest in the knowledge that my November painting is nearly . . . nearly . . . oh, goodness!"

Suddenly realizing the intimate position in which they stood together, Clemma jerked away from him with a gasp. As the heat rushed to her face, she dropped the basket of oranges and clapped her hands over her cheeks and eyes. Turning in dismay, she scrambled away from the easel and started down the path that led to the conservatory door. What had she done? Chatting with him, allowing him to flatter her painting, welcoming his arm about her . . . oh, dear!

"Mrs. Laird!"

He was coming after her, but all she could think was to get away, far away from this place and the man who had so unsettled her.

"Mrs. Laird, I beg you, wait!" He quickly closed in on her and caught her hand. "Please accept my sincerest apologies. I had no intention . . . none whatsoever . . . of upsetting you. I meant nothing untoward. I was merely taken with amazement by your art. I collect art, you see," he rushed on, "and I have some fine pieces displayed at Nasmyth Manor. Watercolors, in fact, for that is the medium which most pleases me. I realize oil is considered superior by some, but I cannot believe it truly captures the living spirit of the landscape, and therefore, I am in the greatest awe of . . . of . . . dear Mrs. Laird, please believe me that I would not distress you for all the world."

Breathing hard, she nodded. "Please release my hand, Dr. Baine. Please go away now."

He dropped her hand and stepped backward. "Forgive me. Clearly, I forgot myself." He bowed. "I shall just collect the oranges and be off."

Clemma stood rigid with dismay as he walked away from her down the path. What had she done? And why did she constantly fall prey to this man's charms? And what on earth was she to do next? Oh, she wished she could hide herself forever! Yet his words of praise continued to drift through her head, and the pressure of his arm around her shoulders lingered on. How good it had felt to know again the easy conversation and warm friendship between a man and a woman. But how very wrong! He was wicked, wicked—she must not forget that!

"Excuse me, Mrs. Laird," Paul Baine said in a low voice as he approached with the basket of oranges. "Might I beg permission to ask you one further question regarding your art?"

Clemma gulped down a breath, nearly choking herself. *No,* she wanted to cry. *No more questions! No more pleasant conversation! Go away, and do not be any part of my life!*

Finally, she nodded.

"You mentioned that this particular painting was your November picture. May I assume, then, that there are others which reflect the flora of the remaining months?"

"Yes, sir," she whispered.

"And where are those?"

"At home. At Brooking House, not far from Longley Park. I live there with my parents."

"Surely such art must not be kept hidden away. You must display these works, Mrs. Laird, for it would be a crime to deny the public the opportunity to reflect upon such beauty."

"Yes, there is a plan . . . I mean to say, no, of course my art is not worthy of such high praise. But there will be a small reception on Christmas Eve in the church hall. An exhibition, you understand, and a printer from London has been invited, a Mr. Street, for I am hoping . . . well, that is enough about the matter."

"But this is a very good plan. I must offer you my warmest congratulations. If your other paintings are as fine as this one, they are worthy of praise indeed. A book is a fine idea, Mrs. Laird, a way to make the collection available to the public—and you must accept my fondest wishes for the success of that venture. Immediately upon its publication, I assure you, the book will be in my possession."

"You flatter me."

"No, madam, my words are not hollow praise. Believe me when I tell you that I have made a dili-

gent study of fine art. I am often compelled to leave
Nasmyth and travel about England and abroad for a
refreshment of my spirit. During those sojourns, I
make every attempt to purchase the highest quality
watercolor paintings available on the market. Yours
are of equal or superior workmanship to any in my
personal collection."

"Oh," she said, unable to bring herself to look
at him.

"And now I bid you good day, Mrs. Laird."

"Good day, Dr. Baine." As he made his way
toward the door, she watched him go, and it
occurred to her again how very gentlemanlike he
seemed, and how very lonely, and how very much
his hair wanted a little trim.

Paul did not wish to return again to the conservatory at Longley Park. He had made a fool of himself
the week before, bumbling about and blathering
over Clementine Laird's painting skills. Worse, it
was eminently clear that she had heard the persistent
rumors about his medical practices. She understood
his reputation, and naturally she could allow herself
only a modicum of civility toward him.

As he tied his horse to the iron fence outside the
conservatory, he shook his head. No, he did not

wish to come, and yet he was here. Nor had he arrived on a Sunday, when he could be certain to avoid Clemma. Instead, he had waited and watched over Alice. Though pleased at his patient's gradual recovery, he found himself constantly recalling another woman's bright blue eyes, fair skin, and pretty blush. Such art that flowed from her slender hand! Truly, Clemma was no ordinary creature. She had been gifted with a talent that surpassed even her own awareness of it.

But he knew. He knew what high praise her paintings should earn. As he stepped through the door and into the conservatory, he acknowledged how greatly he longed to be in her presence again—to watch her paint, to hear her thoughts, to see the kindness in her spirit. Yes, she was kind, even though she knew the worst about him. And that, above all, gave him permission to return.

Far down the long path, he observed her standing before the easel. Summoning the courage to approach, he watched as she swished her paintbrush in a glass of water and set it on a sheet of blotting paper. Then she turned from the table and moved across the path to a grove of potted palm trees. As she seated herself upon a wicker chaise longue, he realized that a tray of tea things had been laid out on a low table nearby. Good. This would give him every reason to collect a few oranges and depart immediately without distressing her again.

As he strolled toward her, she lifted her head, and her blue eyes focused on him. Immediately, a bright pink color flew to her cheeks as she fumbled with the golden twist at the top of her head, tucking in stray wisps here and there. Standing, she cleared her throat and executed a rather awkward curtsy.

"Dr. Baine," she said. "Good afternoon. I had not expected you."

"You are well, Mrs. Laird? Have I disturbed you?"

"No, it is quite all right. I am perfectly fine. Yes, indeed . . . and you?"

"Very well."

"Ah." She twisted her fingers together. "And Alice? How is she?"

"Much better, thank you. I believe you have been praying for her."

"I have."

"And your painting? The November piece?"

"It is nearly done."

"Next must be December. Holly, I suppose? And ivy?"

"Yes, but I am . . ." She seemed flustered, as if unwilling to engage in any but the most shallow of conversations. Clearly his hope for a friendship with Mrs. Laird was in vain. "It is meant to be a collection of flower paintings, you see," she said finally. "Yorkshire flowers. I am desperate for a Christmas Rose, or the entire collection will have to be renamed."

"Is that naughty hellebore still refusing to bloom?" he asked, hoping for a smile. He was rewarded with the very smallest upturn of her mouth, but she kept her eyes averted.

"Not even a bud. I am most disheartened."

"I shall admonish it again on my way to collect the oranges." He stepped toward her easel. "Are they under the table?"

"Yes, but—"

"I shall force myself to avoid looking at your painting. I promise."

Unwilling to detain her any longer from taking tea, he strode across to the area set aside for her painting and knelt to retrieve the basket beneath the table. Seeing Clemma again, he realized how utterly impossible was his fascination with the young woman. She was far too good for him. Far too pure and refined. It was miraculous that she deigned to speak to him at all. How dare he allow himself to think that any woman—let alone one so near perfection as Clementine Laird—might accord him the slightest courtesy?

These must be the last oranges he would fetch from Longley Park, he told himself as he rose with the basket in his arms. Now that Alice was so nearly recovered, he could apportion the fruit more conservatively. By the time these oranges had been consumed, she surely would be well again—and her baby born. His baby. He must not forget that blessed truth, for it was all that could matter to him now.

"Thank you, Mrs. Laird," he said with a bow that enabled him to avoid her eyes. "I shall make every attempt to—"

"Dr. Baine?" She was speaking breathlessly, knotting her fingers as her complexion faded to an ashen gray. "Dr. Baine . . . oh, I am sorry, were you saying something?"

"Just that I shall try to avoid—"

"Would you . . . that is . . . tea . . . would you like to stay to tea?" She waved a nervous hand over the tray. "The pot is quite warm, and you have been out in the cold air. Cook has made a very nice gingerbread here. I know you will like it because she always uses a pound of treacle and all sorts of lovely spices. You do like treacle?"

"Very much."

"And we have several toast sandwiches layered with cold meats of various sorts, all of which are quite delicious. And two crumpets and clotted cream, and I believe this is strawberry jam made from berries grown right in this conservatory, and of course—"

"I should be delighted to stay to tea, Mrs. Laird," he said. "Thank you for honoring me with such an invitation."

For the first time, a true smile lit up her face, though he could not imagine what had brought it on. Surely she must not welcome his presence at her tea table. If anyone saw them together—Hedgley, the gardener, or one of the art students—her own pristine reputation would be sullied by any connection with him. Yet she was indicating a wicker chair near the chaise, and as he sat down, she immediately poured two cups of tea.

"So, Dr. Baine," she said, handing him one, "do tell me about your watercolor collection. It must be fascinating."

Stirring his tea as he pondered the question, Paul wondered whether this discussion was the real reason Clemma had asked him to stay. Or did something else lie beneath the unexpected invitation?

"In my collection of English artists, I own a David Roberts watercolor," he said. "It is from his Egyptian period."

"Egypt? My goodness, I cannot imagine being brave enough to go to Egypt to paint."

"Have you not seen Roberts' work?"

"No, I have not. I have never been to London nor to any of the famous galleries, and Leeds is hardly a center of fine art. The only paintings I really have opportunity to observe are those exe-cuted by the artists residing at Longley Park, and they are mostly done in oil."

"Oil is all very well, but it cannot produce the outstanding depth and sense of light in a painting such as Thomas Rowlandson's seaside village. I have one of his watercolors, and I stand in awe of that man's talent. I also possess a very small watercolor by John Constable—"

"Oh, I have heard of him!"

"Who has not? But my favorite work is actually an etching in combination with watercolor by William Blake. Do you know the man?"

"He is a poet, I believe. My father often recites lines of his verse."

"Poetry, as well as art. Quite accomplished in several areas. His paintings are mostly religious in nature. He took it upon himself to illustrate the entire book of Job, and I am in possession of one of those watercolors."

"Job? I cannot imagine your painting is any plea-sure to view. That is such a sad passage of Scripture. Job lost all his children, his livestock, his crops—everything, you know—and all because Satan asked God to let him test the poor man's faith. I confess, I have always wondered about that. Certainly, I should not like to have Satan meddling about in my life to such an extent."

He regarded her carefully and realized the sincerity behind her statement. "Do you believe in Satan then?" he asked. "A devil, so to speak."

"Of course I do, for how else can one explain the presence of evil in this world?"

"Human nature, I suppose."

"True, we are wicked at heart." She took a sip of tea, as if to avoid looking at him. "Yet I have no doubt that the evil one is behind every misdeed."

"Do you believe me wicked, Mrs. Laird?" he asked in a low voice.

"We are all of us sinners," she said softly, "though Mr. Hedgley reminded me that most of us do not make a regular practice of evildoing."

"But I do?"

She took another drink of tea. He could see that her hands trembled on the cup. "I have heard, sir, of your practice."

"And you find me contemptible."

"Quite the contrary, actually. Which is why it is most difficult for me to reconcile the gentleman who sits at my tea table with the . . . the beast . . . who murders unborn babies."

Stung, Paul felt a fiery rage burst into flame inside his chest. It was just this sort of prejudice and hatred that had exiled him from society! These Christians professed such love and forgiveness—yet they reviled him and made him an outcast! He had no need to sit here any longer and be called a beast by this . . . this . . .

"Can you tell me, sir," Clemma asked, her blue eyes gazing gently upon his face, "how you came to choose this life?"

Slightly calmed by the tenderness in her voice, he took a deep breath. He would relate the sequence of events, though he knew it was a futile exercise. She would never be sympathetic to his abominations.

"My father was a wealthy man," he began, "and when I was still very young, he sent me away from Nasmyth Manor to be trained as a physician. While I was gone from home, my parents both died—and with them, my only source of consultation and advice. Their own pride and high self-regard had kept them estranged from the society in Otley, and therefore, I had no one to befriend me when I returned to our village to begin my medical practice."

"I am very sorry," she said, laying her hand over his. "I have always had a loving family to guide and comfort me."

"It was a loss I was soon to feel most acutely. One evening not long after I had posted a notice that I was available for medical assistance, I received a knock on my door. An elderly woman and her husband entered my office and seated themselves before my desk. With many tears and great agitation, they told me that the woman was expecting a baby—it would be her nineteenth child. To my astonishment, they informed me that seventeen of the children had lived, though the last had died during birth, nearly taking the life of the mother as well."

"Seventeen lived? Such a great number! That is quite unheard of."

"But so it was. The husband was a poor tenant farmer, and with seventeen offspring to feed and clothe, he felt himself drawing near to insanity. It seemed certain to them both that he must soon be placed in a debtors' prison. Furthermore, they expressed such fear that the woman would perish during the birth of this baby, leaving all her other children motherless, that I found myself agreeing to something that was far beyond my intent as a physician." He hesitated a moment. "I did—as you say—murder their unborn child."

Expecting a hard look of reproach on her face, Paul was surprised to find that Clemma was weeping. She took a handkerchief from her sleeve and blotted her cheek.

"It was very wrong of you," she said, "and yet, I can see how you were drawn into the desperation of such a dire situation."

"Not long after that event—and before I had

been able to establish a practice in the village—another woman came to me, accompanied by her mother. The girl's entire body was swollen with fluid, and she was clearly near to death. Her mother begged me on her knees to spare the life of her daughter by ridding her of the unwanted pregnancy. Once again, I did so."

"Oh, dear."

"By that time, my reputation in Otley was established, and I was shunned wherever I went. Gradually, I lost all feeling, all sense of conscience about my actions. The only thing that held my interest was the propagation of my roses and the other plants in my own small conservatory. I began to experiment with tonics and compresses and various formulas to ease the suffering of my patients. Somehow along the way, I created a salve that I found successful in tempering the ravages of the sexually acquired diseases with which many of my patients were afflicted. Word of this went out, and suddenly sailors and other men suffering those same plagues began to appear at Nasmyth. I took their money—as much of it as I could—and away they went with their healing creams."

Bitter at the retelling of his own story, Paul set down his cup and made to rise. "And now you know, Mrs. Laird, how the devil came to play with me, as he played with poor old Job."

She caught his arm. "Dr. Baine," she said, "I thank you for your honesty. The path you have chosen is wrong, but at least I understand how you came to walk upon it."

"You understand, perhaps, yet you would not have been so weak, so susceptible to the devil's wiles?"

"I was not attacked as you were."

"You were not attacked at all!" he said derisively. "You have your family, your lovely home, your paintings—"

"I lost my husband, my house, my future," she said. "We had a fire. I am not unscathed, Dr. Baine."

Startled, he realized he had been thinking only of his own suffering. "I did not know."

"And yet it is true. Satan was allowed to play with me just a little. I bear the scars of his touch."

Paul looked into Clemma's tear-filled blue eyes and felt certain that he could not remain another moment. He defiled her with his presence.

"And yet you kept your faith in God," he said, standing and pulling away from her. "Like Job, you never wavered. I, on the other hand, am a Judas Iscariot."

Without waiting for her response, he snatched up the basket of oranges and fled the conservatory.

FOUR

"I AIN'T SEEN 'IM about these days," Mr. Hedgley said as he lifted a watering can and soaked an array of pink begonias. "Good thing, eh? Ye got rid of 'im."

Clemma gazed forlornly at the stubbornly barren Christmas Rose on her little table. "He has not come back, that is true. But I can assure you, he is most welcome should he need more oranges."

"Welcome? Dr. Baine?" The gardener's fluffy white eyebrows raised in surprise. "Now wot would make a lady say such a thing about a man like 'im?"

"Paul Baine is very bad, but I cannot hate him. I have found that the moment one knows the human condition, the reason for sin, the abhorrent road down which one's fellowman has stumbled, one can no longer despise him."

"I can despise 'im, all right. 'e kills babies. Wot greater monster can there be, Mrs. Laird, I ask ye?"

"He is like this hellebore," she sighed.

"Refusin' to bloom?"

Clemma shook her head. "Mr. Hedgley, have you ever seen the root of a Christmas Rose? It is black—as black as the wicked, cold heart of a demon. And it is filled with the most violent poison."

"Poison!"

"Indeed. To prepare for my December painting, I read about *Helleborus niger* in the great library at Longley Park. A drop of poison from its root can completely stupefy a man. Delirium and insanity are common effects, as are vertigo, vomiting, and dreadful pain. Some have used the plant in witchcraft—"

"Nay! Not that!"

"They believe it will make them invisible or able to fly. Yet there can be no doubt that this illusion is caused by the visions which the poison induces. In short, Mr. Hedgley, the *Helleborus niger* is a most villainous plant."

The old fellow regarded the small pot with its evergreen leaves, and a gradual frown turned down the corners of his mouth. He peered at the plant, he squinted his eyes, and finally, he picked it up and set off down the path.

"Mr. Hedgley!" Clemma cried, racing after him. "Where are you taking my hellebore?"

"Outside to t' burnin' pit where it belongs. Nothin' like this 'as a place in me conservatory, I assure ye that!"

"Wait, I beg you." She caught his elbow and forced him to stop. "Please let me finish my story, for I was comparing the Christmas Rose to Dr. Baine."

"Aye, and ye done such a good job of it that I'm sorely tempted to tie t' both of 'em to a stake and set 'em afire!"

"But there is much more to the hellebore, Mr. Hedgley. True, the nature of the plant is vile—but by the grace of God it has become a thing of great beauty! It is called the Holy Night Rose, the Rose of Noel, and Christ's Bloom. Have you ever heard the legend of the Christmas Rose?"

"No, I ain't." He set the plant on a marble pedestal and glared at it. "Wot legend?"

"It is said that a young girl named Madelon followed the shepherds to the manger in Bethlehem on Christmas night. She was very poor and had no gift to offer the Christ child. Standing outside the stable, she was weeping, when suddenly the angel Gabriel appeared before her and asked the cause of her distress. As she told him of her sorrow, he touched his staff to the frozen ground where her tears had fallen. And immediately there sprang up the exquisite white blossoms of the Christmas Rose."

Mr. Hedgley gave a grunt. "A pretty tale, but I still think t' plant deserves a burnin'."

"Indeed, it does. But can you not see, sir, how the touch of God can transform anything? How God's love can make even the most reprehensible things into beings that are pure and useful and utterly beautiful? God can change a vile plant . . . and he can change a wicked man."

The old gardener's rheumy eyes focused on Clemma. "God can do wonders, dear lady, that I know. But at t' very 'eart of t' matter, that plant still 'as got a poisonous root. And that Dr. Baine 'as got t' blackest soul of any man in Yorkshire. Ye mark my words."

So saying, he turned on his heel and set off for the door. Clemma gazed after him, unable to deny that what he said was true. Dr. Baine had shown no sign of remorse for his evil deeds. No evidence of repentance. He never set foot in the church, and he had admitted that he never prayed. Certainly God could change him. But he wouldn't without an invitation from the man himself.

Distraught as the reality of the predicament swept over her, Clemma left the hellebore on the pedestal and walked back to her easel. She stared at the sketch of cascading ivy, prickly holly, and her rough attempt to capture what she remembered of a

Christmas Rose. Then she looked down at the basket of oranges and lemons she had been gathering over such a long time.

Where was he? Why had he not come back? On his last visit, she had spontaneously invited him to tea, trying to demonstrate that she did not disdain him. Trying to be used of God, for it was clear that her heavenly Father had brought Paul Baine into her life. But Paul had told her about his terrible past, run away from her, and never returned. Why? Had Clemma said something wrong? Had Alice died? Or been healed? Was Dr. Baine too ashamed to be seen at the conservatory again? Why, oh why, had he not come back!

Clenching her fists, Clemma felt almost as if she were going to explode. What should she do? What action was right and what was wrong? And why did she even care about that black-hearted man?

"Oh, blast!" she said finally, sweeping the basket into her arms and setting off down the path through the conservatory. Fear and loathing and common sense to the contrary, she was going to pay a visit to Nasmyth Manor.

A chill wind swept across the moorlands and down the fells, cutting through the green wool wrap that

covered Clemma's head. Even her gloved fingers
were stiff and painful as she reached for the bellpull
outside the great oak door. It had taken much
longer than she anticipated to walk from Longley
Park to Nasmyth Manor, for the village of Otley lay
on the path.

Reverend Springle, the kindly minister of the
small church in Otley, had happened to spy Clemma
passing by, and he begged her to come into the hall
and make certain there would be space to hang all her
pieces for the Christmas Eve exhibition. *Twelve paintings!* he kept saying, as though they had not measured
the entire room twice before. *Twelve!*

Next he insisted they address the matter of
refreshment, which Clemma already had offered to
provide but which the church ladies had decided
they wished to furnish. And finally, there was a
discussion of decoration for the hall, which
normally during the season was festooned with
hangings of Christmas greenery—ivy, holly, mistletoe, and fir branches. But would these adornments
detract from Clemma's paintings? the minister
wondered. The announcement of the exhibition
had created quite a stir in Otley, Reverend Springle
assured her, and he wanted to make certain that
everything went off without a hitch.

By the time she arrived at Nasmyth Manor,
Clemma had missed her tea altogether, and the hour

was growing toward dinnertime. And now it seemed there were no servants available to answer Dr. Baine's doorbell, for she had rung it many times. Becoming impatient at the delay, she finally gave the handle a turn, and the door swung open into an unlit foyer shrouded in heavy velvet curtains.

"Good afternoon!" she called out. "I say, is anyone at home?"

Feeling nearly frozen through, she stepped into the cavernous room and shut the door behind her. "I beg your pardon, Dr. Baine," she sang out in the most cheerful voice she could muster. "Are you here?"

Though she heard no response, she noticed that a corridor at the top of the long staircase was lit. Surely no one would go away from his home and leave candles burning. Memories of the fire that had reduced her husband's house to ashes so many years before sent a shiver down her spine.

"Dr. Baine!" she cried again. "It is I, Clementine Laird! I am here to call on Alice. I have brought oranges."

Her words echoed up and down the empty foyer, bouncing from the soaring ceiling to the marble floors and back again. No answer came, and yet she sensed that someone was in the house. What if Dr. Baine had taken ill? Or what if someone from the village had come and killed him? Such a thing was too horrible to imagine! But she had no doubt how deeply the man was hated. If Mr. Hedgley—who was kind to everyone and seemed able to forgive almost any sin—despised the doctor, think how everyone else must feel.

Frightened at the image of bloody murder that presented itself in her mind, Clemma summoned up her courage and stepped toward the staircase. Nasmyth Manor must have been grand and glorious at one time, she realized as she mounted the stairs. Large paintings—Dr. Baine's collection of watercolors—and multihued tapestries graced the foyer's walls, and an immense crystal chandelier hung from a golden chain. It might have held a hundred glittering candles at one time, though now there were only cobwebs and dust. At the landing, two magnificent portraits were displayed. Mounted in ornately carved and gilded frames, they clearly depicted Dr. Baine's parents, who had passed on so long ago.

But what a dreary place this was, Clemma thought as she started down the dimly lit corridor. Had it always been this way? Or had it fallen into such a sad state after Dr. Baine began his infamous medical practice? A musty scent clung to the carpet, and some of the wallpaper had rolled right down from the ceiling to hang upon the walls like an old lady's gray ringlets. Shivering, Clemma clutched the basket of oranges tightly. An eerie veil of gloom lay over the house, and she could not prevent herself from thinking of all the poor infant souls who had lost their lives in this dreadful place.

As she made a turn in the hallway, a cry suddenly rang out. The wail drifted down the empty corridor, wrapped around the candle sconces, and lifted the hair at the back of Clemma's neck. At that moment, a door opened somewhere beyond her; then it shut with a bang. A stale gust of air swept across the candles and snuffed out the flames.

Trembling, Clemma backed up against the wall and held her breath, as if she could somehow make herself invisible. Were there ghosts in this place? Did spirits of unborn babies haunt these halls? Her mouth dry, she clung to her basket and tried to force air down into her lungs. No, that was silly, she told herself. Ghosts did *not* exist.

And then again—another cry drifted down, this one coming from overhead in the opposite direction. It was a high-pitched wail, like the forlorn weeping of an abandoned child, and the sound of it pricked goose bumps on Clemma's arms. *Goodness gracious!* Nearly dropping the oranges in her haste to flee, she picked up her skirts and rounded the darkened corner. And in that instant, she collided full force with something enormous and very solid. The basket hit the floor and oranges began rolling down the steps. Clemma grabbed for the stair rail to keep from tumbling herself, but her hand closed instead on a large bare arm, heavily sinewed and covered with hair. An ogre! A monster!

"Oh, heaven help me," she cried as the creature clamped its horrible hands on her shoulders. "I beg you, do not hurt me, for I mean no harm at all, and I am truly just leaving if only you will let go of my—"

"Mrs. Laird?" The voice was filled with astonishment. "Is it you?"

Breathing hard, she attempted to keep from swooning. "I . . . I am just going away now—"

"Mrs. Laird . . . but it is I, Paul Baine." The figure stepped away from her, and in a moment the candles in a nearby sconce flickered to life. "You appear most unwell, dear lady. Do allow me to escort you—"

"One moment, please." She held up her hand. "Permit me to recover myself."

Gracious, what a start he had given her, she thought as her heart began to resume its regular rhythm. Had Paul Baine always been so prodigiously large? In the vastness of the conservatory, he had not seemed so, but now she realized that he was tall, broad-shouldered, and well muscled. Wearing a white shirt with the sleeves rolled nearly to the elbows, gray wool trousers, and nothing but socks on his feet, he appeared discomfortingly homey . . . even normal . . . and handsome . . .

"I brought oranges." Clemma spoke quickly,

concerned that her cheeks might be flushing at the thoughts that swirled through her head. "For Alice. You did not come back to the conservatory, you see, and I thought, well, perhaps I should bring the oranges here just in case something had happened to you, because . . . because I had not seen you in such a great many days that . . . well, you can imagine."

Oddly, he was smiling at her, and Clemma realized that she had not seen such a nice smile in a very long time. How disconcerting to be discovered on the second floor of someone's home—as though she had been creeping about like a thief. She should not have come. The house had ghosts in the corridors, strange slamming doors, and a most unsettling master.

"Thank you very much indeed," he said. "Though I fear the oranges have gone off down the stairs with a mind of their own."

"I shall just go and collect them again."

"Wait." He held out a hand. "I must tell you first how grateful I am that you took it upon yourself to come all this distance."

"It is not so very far." Glancing at him, she found it utterly dismaying to discover that he did not look villainous at all. Instead, he resembled a much younger version of her dear papa! With a pair of spectacles perched on his nose and an old cardigan, he would have been a perfectly ordinary, commonplace, comfortable—

A distant cry silenced Clemma's thoughts. Another ghost? Stiffening, she saw Dr. Baine look upward in the direction of the sound. So he heard it, too. And that was when her focus fell upon his hands.

"Your fingers!" she gasped.

He looked down, as if seeing them for the first time.

"What have you done?" Clemma backed up against the banister. "Your hands are . . . are covered in blood!"

Stifling a scream, she started down the stairs. But he came after her, calling out, reaching for her with his crimsoned hands.

"No, Clementine, wait!" he called. "It is not what you think. I promise you. I swear it!"

"You are a murderer!"

"No!"

"Some innocent—"

"Clemma, please!" He caught her wrist. "I have never lied to you, and I do not lie now. There has been no death!"

"But your hands—"

"I have not killed anyone. You must believe me. Please, I beg you to trust me."

"Oh, Dr. Baine," she cried, her eyes filling with tears. "I want to trust you. I long to believe the best of you. But your guilty stains are visible for me and everyone else to see!"

"I am guilty of many things, Clemma, that is true. Yet, not everything is what it may seem to be." He relaxed his hold on her arm. "Will you come with me? May I show you something?"

Clemma glanced down at the foyer, wishing she could escape through that door and never come to this place again. How she longed to be curled up beside the fire at Brooking House—Mama crocheting snowflakes for the Christmas tree and Papa reading aloud some endless passage from his beloved John Milton. Oh, for a cup of hot tea and a nice slice of buttered toast and a long letter from one of her sisters.

"Please," he whispered. "You are the first . . . the only person in many years to treat me as a human being. Your kindness . . . your charity . . . your honesty . . . dearest lady, you mean more to me than anyone I have ever known, and I would never do anything to hurt or betray you. You must believe that."

Bloody hands, the dark pall of death, a house echoing with the cries of unborn souls—everything shouted at Clemma to run. *Run!*

But she could not. Once she, too, had lived in a place of hopelessness and despair. She remembered well the months following her husband's death, the burning of their home, the injuries she had suffered. Yet she had been surrounded by the warmth and love of Mama, Papa, and countless friends. More important, she knew the hand of God had never left her, and her faith had been more than sufficient to sustain her through the dark days.

Who did this man have? she wondered, searching his face. Who would ever give him a chance?

"I shall follow you," she said softly. "You may show me whatever you like."

With a look of gratitude, he turned away in silence and led her up the staircase again and along the dimly lit hall. As they passed the sconce, he lifted out a candle and carried it around the corner to a door at the far end of the wing. Clemma's heart hammered like Otley's blacksmith on his anvil. Yet she forced herself to follow Paul Baine into that unknown room.

"Mrs. Laird," he said, stepping aside, "I should like you to meet Alice."

Clemma approached a large bed fitted with fine blue brocade hangings and piled with snowy white pillows. Upon them lay a young woman whose great brown eyes flickered open to gaze at the stranger in her room.

"Alice," Dr. Baine said, "this is Mrs. Clementine Laird, the lady who has kindly provided us with oranges and lemons from Longley Park."

Alice's face lightened. "Welcome, madam," she

said. "She has come just in time, eh, Dr. Baine?
'ave a look then, me lady."

So saying, she turned down the edge of the sheet
to reveal a small, round, pink face—a tiny, wrinkled
raisin of a face with the frown of a little old man
and a head pointed like an elf's. Clemma gaped.

"This be Mary Elizabeth," Alice said. "Just
birthed and near as wore out from it as poor Dr.
Baine and me."

"We have had quite a time of it," Dr. Baine
added. "Alice labored more than two days, and I
greatly feared we should lose both her and the child."

"Without them oranges and lemons, I could not
of done it, Mrs. Laird. I ain't got but three teeth
left in me 'ead, and me joints still ache, but t' scurvy
'as loosed its claws from me body. I am grateful to
ye, most grateful indeed."

Still unable to make herself speak, Clemma
stared at the tiny newborn. A bruised head and
swollen eyes gave testament to the difficulty the child
had endured. Yet her rosebud mouth and slender
fingers promised a sweet beauty in the years to
come.

"I had just carried the birthing implements
down to the kitchen," Dr. Baine explained, "and I
was returning to make certain all was well with
mother and child before taking my leave to wash up,
when I encountered you in the corridor."

Clemma's focus darted to his bloody hands as a trickle of understanding ran down her spine. "You delivered the baby," she murmured. "But . . . but I thought you . . . you were—"

"No longer. That aspect of my medical practice ended long ago."

"Long ago? You did not tell me. You allowed me to berate and accuse you, and yet you knew what I said was wrong."

"Not wrong. I once did everything of which you accused me. I committed the vilest of deeds, just as I told you. When we spoke at tea in the conservatory, I gave the entire account of my life with accuracy, though I did not take the time to acquaint you of the changes I have made in the past years."

"But whyever not?" A strange warmth began to creep into Clemma's heart. "You have ceased those infamous deeds, and you are now washed clean of them!"

"Clean? I think not." He reached down and stroked the infant's head. "I do not know if I can ever atone for the enormity of my wrongdoings. I only know that not long after I had performed those first procedures, I came to my senses. I saw that if I were to continue in such a path, my life would become hopeless and my conscience would be so suppressed as to make me truly evil. But as it has turned out, my early actions continue to haunt me, and it seems little can be done to alter the bleak course of my existence."

"Oh, Dr. Baine!"

"Please, my name is Paul. I believe we are beyond such formalities now, for you know every secret part of my life." He tucked the sheet under the baby's chin. "Allow me to wash up, Mrs. Laird—"

"Clementine," she corrected him. "Or Clemma."

"Clemma," he repeated. "Then I shall show you my infirmary and the residential ward."

As he turned to a washbasin and began to scrub his hands with soap and water, Clemma stepped closer to the bed. Alice's eyes opened again, and she gave her visitor a weary smile.

"Your baby is lovely, Alice. I'm sure your husband will be most delighted to see Mary Elizabeth when you return with her to Hull."

"Oh, I ain't got no 'usband, Mrs. Laird." She shrugged. "And I won't be takin' Mary back 'ome with me, neither. She'll be stayin' right 'ere at Nasmyth Manor. 'ere with 'er papa." At this, she tilted her chin toward the man at the basin. "Dr. Baine is t' child's father. 'e wants 'er to live with 'im at Nasmyth Manor."

"*His* child?" Clemma managed to whisper.

"Aye, but—"

"Well, then! Let me just have another look at you, my dear." Dr. Baine stepped up to the bed.

Bending over, he peered into Alice's eyes and pulled down her lips to check her mouth. "I shall bring orange juice within the hour. We must not cease the treatment until we are absolutely certain the scurvy has vanished entirely. And now, Clemma, will you accompany me?"

Feeling as though she had just been spun about by a cream whisk, Clemma followed him back into the corridor. *Dear God, what is happening?* she prayed. At first, Paul Baine had been a black-souled villain with no remorse for his murderous deeds. Then he became a repentant man who used his skill to bring life into the world rather than to destroy it. And now to find he was the father of a baby girl born to an unwed mother.

Had he no morals? Did he not know how to behave as a gentleman ought? Had his parents sent him away to school so early in life that he was given no ethical compass?

"This is the infirmary," Paul said, pushing open a door that led into a series of large rooms, each containing two or three beds. Moving from one patient to another, he spoke in a low voice. "This is Jack. He suffers an advanced stage of syphilis. Morphine is the only remedy, I fear. Here is Ted. He accidentally cut off most of his hand while building a ship. I had treated him earlier for a different condition, and he returned to stay with me while his hand heals. I find I have had some success in preventing infection in such grave wounds."

At each bed, Paul paused, laid a hand on his patient's forehead or shoulder, and spoke a few words of comfort. Then he led Clemma into the women's ward. There, she found several patients with life-threatening diseases and two in the later stages of a difficult pregnancy.

"I urge them to stay at Nasmyth Manor," he explained as he led Clemma up a flight of stairs. "If they remained at home, they would have no choice but to continue cooking, caring for their other children, even working at the worsted mills or fisheries. Here, they can rest until their children are safely born."

Filled with wonder at this statement from a man known as a baby killer, Clemma entered an enormous room at the top of the stairs. To her utter shock, the area was abustle with women, several small children, and two newborn infants. No wonder she had heard wails echoing through the house!

"Good evening, ladies," Paul said as he approached a cluster of very young ladies who looked ready to deliver at any moment. "Jane, how are you feeling?"

A fragile young blonde looked away with an embarrassed giggle. "I'm right well, sir."

"Don't listen to 'er, Dr. Baine," a redhead with

a hearty sprinkling of freckles retorted. "She's been laborin' all afternoon. If we don't 'ave a baby by midnight, I'll eat me own bonnet."

The women laughed as Paul drew Clemma forward. "Mrs. Laird, this is the residential ward. These ladies have come to spend the latter weeks of their confinement at Nasmyth Manor."

"Latter weeks?" the redhead said. "I been 'ere nearly t' whole time. I come to Dr. Baine fer 'elp when I learned I were to 'ave a baby. I wanted to get rid of it, fearin' me papa would beat me to death if he knew what I done, me not married an' all. But t' doctor said 'e wouldn't 'elp me—'e didn't do that kind of medicine no more. I were right put off, don't ye know? But then 'e told me I could stay 'ere at Nasmyth till t' baby come, and 'e'd find a good 'ome for it. So 'ere I be!"

When Clemma looked at Paul in confusion, he explained. "After making my decision to refuse any more surgeries of the sort I could no longer bear to perform, I found that women in trouble continued to come to me for assistance. At first, I turned them away. But while I was staying in London on business, a barrister mentioned that he and his wife had been unable to have children of their own. I asked him if he would be willing to adopt a baby should I provide one born of a healthy woman. He assured me that this would be a splendid solution to his problem."

"Oh, my!" Clemma said, realizing what was to come.

"I returned home," Paul continued, "and convinced one of the women who had come to destroy her child to instead stay at Nasmyth until the baby was born. She willingly surrendered the infant upon its birth, knowing her son would go to a good home. Then I drove back to London and presented my friend the barrister and his wife with a delightful baby boy. Within a few weeks, I began to receive many requests for infants from others of his acquaintance. Word of this happy connection spread among those unable to bear children—and also among those unable to care for the ones they were bearing already. Now women come to me for their confinement, confident that I will assure their babies a good future."

"In short," Clemma said, "you have found a way to provide a service to these women and to those families without children."

"Exactly."

"But this is marvelous! Why have you told no one of this? Surely your reputation must be recovered, and your medical practice restored, and your entire life made commendable!"

"Life is not so neatly tied up in pretty packages, is it, dearest lady?" he asked, leading her out of the room again. "Because you are good at heart, you assume the same of others. Because you can forgive, you believe others will forgive as well. But I fear I know the dark soul of man far better than you, my dear Clemma. I have seen the hardness there, the propensity toward evil, the bitterness and hatred."

"Surely you cannot think you would be shunned if people knew the change in you?" Walking beside him down the long flights of steps, she grasped at thin threads of hope. "People are not so unforgiving, are they?"

"I believe they are, madam." He picked up the basket where Clemma had dropped it and started down to the foyer. "But it is not the people of Otley or any other town or city in England whose good opinion I seek. I long ago ceased to care what people thought of me. Most of my servants fled, I have been spat upon, even attacked and beaten. I no longer care how the human race feels about me."

"Then why have you made this change? Whose good opinion do you seek?"

"God's." He escorted her to the door. "I have no doubt of his existence, you see. No man who has witnessed the wonders of the human body, as I have, could deny the presence of a divine Creator. And I spent enough years in the tutelage of those who believe in Jesus Christ to accept that he was God's Son. In this much, I suppose, I am a Christian."

"Well, but I think—"

"Yet I shall never set foot in a church," he

continued, "and never associate myself with those blind and prejudiced people who claim that title. No, it is only God's forgiveness and acceptance that I seek. And therefore, by these means which you have observed, I shall continue my efforts to atone for my past wrongdoings. And when I die, perhaps I shall be considered good enough to enter into the presence of God. It is the afterlife, then, that I look forward to with great anticipation. This present life, dear Clemma, holds no hope of joy."

With those final words, he opened the door and led her out into the evening. "Unless you object," he said, "I shall take you home in my carriage. Your parents must be concerned at your long absence."

Clemma consented, grateful to be spared a walk in the growing darkness. But her efforts to resume the conversation during the ride home were futile. He would hear nothing. He would say nothing. The topic was entirely closed.

And so they discussed the Christmas Rose and the hope Clemma yet nurtured that a tiny bud might soon emerge among its evergreen leaves.

FIVE

To Paul's surprise and delight, Clemma returned to Nasmyth Manor the following day and nearly every day after that. With a zeal he had not expected, she tossed aside her cultured upbringing and set to work on a miraculous transformation of his household. Floors were scrubbed, sheets washed, and window-panes shined. The most sumptuous meals Paul had tasted in many years were served up. Clemma was not so much the laborer herself as the grand orchestra conductor, marshaling into service the ladies in the residence ward.

If they were at all able to work, she handed them mops, buckets, dust rags, silver polish, and oil. She opened every room on the first floor—parlors, drawing rooms, dining rooms, the billiards room, the game room, and the foyer. Curtains slid back, carpets rolled up and went out into the chill December air for a good beating, tables and mantelpieces shed years of dust and cobwebs. New candles appeared in sconces and chandeliers. Fresh flowers from the Longley conservatory blossomed in countless vases and epergnes. And food— mountains of food—began arriving at the kitchen door in the carts of vegetable sellers, butchers, and fishmongers. Mrs. Clementine Laird, it seemed, had ordered the shopkeepers in Otley to begin making regular deliveries to Nasmyth Manor again, and she would brook no refusal.

"In fact," she told Paul one afternoon as they sat at tea beside a roaring fire in the drawing room, "as quickly as evil rumors about you were spread, rumors of your transformation are taking their place. Indeed, Mr. Hedgley told me just yesterday that his grandson might be asking you for a position as head gardener here at Nasmyth. Can you imagine? Mr. Hedgley wanted nothing to do with you only three weeks ago, and now his grandson hopes to work for you. Which, by the by, I think you should allow, for he has been trained by the finest gardener in Yorkshire. In Mr. Hedgley there is no better groundskeeper, and I am sure his grandson could do wonders with your own gardens and hothouse."

As Clemma paused in her excited chatter to take

a sip of tea, Paul gazed in wonder at her golden hair. How had he been given such a glorious gift as the friendship of this woman? He did not deserve her. He deserved nothing—neither the flowers nor the food nor the clean house. And he certainly did not merit the immense pleasure of Clemma's cheery "good morning" each day, her bright blue eyes, and her undying generosity of spirit. If he had been able to deny his growing attachment to the lovely artist before, he could do so no longer. Try as he might, he could not suppress a longing, a small hope, that she might one day feel the same.

"Did you know that Lizzy and Bess have asked to stay on here after their babies are born?" she asked. "And as Bess lives in Otley and Lizzy's papa owns a cottage not two miles from Nasmyth Manor, I do think you ought to take them on. It would be no great inconvenience for them to come and go, and as you well know, Lizzy is a marvel in the kitchen. I believe you complimented her fig pudding only yesterday, for it was remarkably delicious. Truly, if the choice were up to me, I should make her next in line for the position of head cook. She is young but very eager, and what more could you ask? Besides, she has been taught to read a little bit, and such a skill is ever so helpful in following recipes. Our cook at Brooking House cannot read a word, and it is left to the footman to read recipes to her. He despises it, as you can imagine."

"Yes, indeed," Paul said, fighting the urge to chuckle. How light and joy-filled his world had become! And he knew every good thing in his life could be traced to Clemma. He could not imagine how he had survived so many years without her.

With each passing hour, the faint hope grew stronger in his heart. Could she ever care enough for him to learn to love him? Was it possible that she might be willing to take his hand in marriage, to be his wife, to live with him forever?

"You will want a good tutor for Mary Elizabeth," she was saying now, oblivious to the growing desire in her companion's chest. "I used to believe that all a lady needed was to become accomplished in the feminine arts—needlework, painting, and decoupage. Of course, it is always helpful to know how to play at whist, to be able to entertain guests on the pianoforte, and to recollect the rules of croquet. And a lady must have some skill in managing a household. But now I am certain that reading is important, too. The pleasures of a good book cannot be denied, and Mary Elizabeth must learn her mathematics as well."

Paul set his teacup on the table, wondering if he might find some way to test the heart of this woman he had come to adore so deeply. "You seem quite content with the knowledge of my relationship to Alice's daughter," he said. "It does not trouble you that I would choose to keep the child here?"

"No, not at all. You are her father, and it is right of you to make her your heir."

"You believe that Alice and I created this child, and yet you do not condemn me?"

Suddenly blushing, Clemma pretended to study the fire for a moment. "In learning to know you, Paul, I have also learned not to judge. I cannot approve of the circumstances in which the child was conceived. To be frank, I find the situation abhorrent—yet I refuse to condemn you, Alice, or the baby. It is not my place."

"What is your place here, Clemma? Why have you come into my life?"

Her blue eyes darted to his face. "Am I intruding?"

"Hardly. I welcome the sight of you each morning. I mourn your absence from my table each evening. You have become . . . you *are* . . . very precious to me." He paused. "Clemma, I am not the natural father of Mary Elizabeth."

"You are not? But I thought—"

"Alice was living in Hull when she began to show symptoms of scurvy. She had no money for treatment and no idea what was causing her illness. While walking the streets one evening, she was attacked and ravished by a mob of drunken seamen. Of course she had no strength to defend herself against them, and she lay in a ditch for a day and a night before she was discovered there, nearly dead.

On learning of her pregnancy as a result of that attack, her father threw her out of the house. When she came to me for help in ridding herself of the child, she was so ill with scurvy that I could not imagine her survival possible. Equally significant, I knew none of the families awaiting children in London would take a baby conceived under such circumstances."

"But it was not the fault of the child!"

"You can see that, my dear Clemma, but others are not so generous in nature. No, I knew the baby might be born malformed as a result of the mother's poor health. Moreover, this child would never have a home. Indeed, the mother might not survive. Even if she did, she was too poor and weak to care for herself and a newborn."

"Oh, this is a dreadful tale. I had no idea."

"Before Alice came to my doorstep, I had done everything I could to change the course of my life in the hope of atoning for my sins and making peace with God. In agreeing to take Alice's child as my own, I began to believe that I might actually find a measure of happiness. A child . . . a son or daughter . . . a family. Can you understand the appeal of that, Clemma?"

"Yes," she whispered, her eyes misting. "I had hoped . . . once . . . for children of my own. For a family. But . . . but . . ."

"Clemma, my darling," he said, taking her hand, "is there any chance that you and I . . . that there might be hope for us? Could you accept me . . . love me . . . despite what you know of my past? Mary Elizabeth could be your daughter, our daughter! And perhaps one day, there would be others. Children, a home filled with laughter and joy. Clemma, I beg you to tell me my dreams are not in vain. Tell me you love me . . . as I love you."

As tears tumbled down her cheeks, she pulled her hand away from his and stood from the chair. "No," she murmured, her voice barely audible. "I did not come to Nasmyth for this . . . for the hope that you would love me. It was never my intention to care for you."

"Then why did you come?"

"I came because I longed to show you that true love cannot be earned. It is never deserved."

"I know I do not deserve your love, Clemma. I have no illusions about the black stain upon my life."

"I do not speak of my love. I speak of God's love, Paul." She blotted her cheeks with a handkerchief. "In coming here, in befriending you, I hoped you would begin to see that not all Christians are condemning. That some of us do try to walk as Christ teaches us—in forgiveness and love. I wanted you to understand that there is nothing you can do to atone for your sin."

"Nothing I can do? How, then, do I have any hope at all?" He stood to face her. "Look what has happened in my life since I chose to try to win God's approval. I now have a medical practice of which I am not ashamed. I have a baby daughter. And you . . . Clemma, I hoped I had you. No, of course I deserve none of these blessings. But in working hard, in doing everything possible to please God, I have made some headway, have I not?"

"None at all," she said softly. "Oh, Paul, you cannot do enough good things to earn a place in heaven."

"I can certainly try! I am not so far down the ladder to hell that I have no hope at all of climbing back out."

"But we do not get into heaven by climbing a ladder of good deeds."

"Then how can such a thing be accomplished?"

"Heaven, forgiveness, salvation from sin—these are gifts, dearest Paul. They are free. You can do nothing to earn them." She tucked her handkerchief back into her sleeve. "Reverend Springle has spoken of it many times in church, but you have not . . . you have not felt welcome there. My heart breaks that you and these others—your poor patients—are so vilified that you will not come into the sanctuary and hear the words of hope and remission of sin."

"Tell me then," Paul said, his heart troubled.

"What has Reverend Springle said about the way to heaven?"

"There is only one path, and it is through Jesus," she said. "God did not send his Son into the world to condemn it, but to save it. There is no judgment awaiting those who trust Christ. Only those who reject him are judged, for it is clear that they love darkness more than light. Can you see that God accepts us when we surrender our lives to him—not when we have somehow become good enough? It is not good deeds that free us from judgment. It is trust in Jesus."

Paul stood staring at her, confused and dismayed by her words. "This, then, is the reason for your friendship? You made yourself a living allegory of my undeserved acceptance by Christ?"

She nodded, beginning to weep again. "Yes, I confess, at first that was why I befriended you. I wanted to be a model of Christ, and that is all. But then . . . then I began to care for you more personally. I saw you as a man, as a physician, as a loving father to Mary Elizabeth. You have become very precious to me."

"But you will not consider any possibility of a future between us?"

"No," she wept, fumbling for her handkerchief again. "No, I cannot!"

"Why, Clemma? What else can I do?"

"You can do nothing."

"Is it fear of rejection by those you love? Is it your dread of censure by the society in Otley? Does my past yet come between us?"

"Not your past," she cried. "Mine! It is my past that separates us—that must separate us always."

"Yours? What can you mean, darling Clemma? There is nothing—"

"Oh, I must go!"

Grabbing her wool shawl from the settee, she fled the drawing room. He dashed after her, hoping to stop her, longing to understand. But she would not be held back. As powdery snowflakes blew through the open door, she raced outside and vanished in the swirling mist.

※ ※ ※

"It refused to bloom," Clemma said as her mother stood in the church hall and gazed at the December painting. "I had no choice but to copy my Christmas Rose out of the botany books in the library."

Mama shook her head. "I am sorry to tell you this, my sweet Clemma, but I fear there is a certain artificiality to the flower. Perhaps it is too small."

"Too pink," Papa said, peering at the painting through his monocle. "You have got it far too pink, dear girl. The *Helleborus niger* is white, pure white."

"But I am quite sure I recall a pink tinge to the edges of the petals, Papa," Clemma said.

"No, indeed, for they are altogether white."

She blew out a breath of disgust. "I did all I could to bring that stubborn plant into blossom, but it would not listen to me. And now I have got a pink hellebore! The guests are to arrive in minutes, and what will Mr. Street think when he comes all the way from London to view my paintings and sees a pink hellebore. But what could I do? There was no bud!"

"Ah, but there is always a bud, my dear Clemma. For as our own John Keats—God rest his soul—put it so aptly,

'Shed no tear! O shed no tear!
The flower will bloom another year.
Weep no more! O weep no more!
Young buds sleep in the root's white core.'"

"The root of the hellebore is black," Clemma said, "but thank you for the sentiment, Papa. Perhaps I shall have a blossom one day and can paint away this flower and paint in another."

"There!" Mama agreed. "A wise plan. One must never give up hope for better things."

Clemma turned away from her flawed picture as the mayor of Otley, followed by many of his constituents, stepped into the hall. In some things, she reminded herself as she went to greet her guests, one must not hold out any hope. Better things were not always possible, no matter how much one wished they might be.

"I say, have you tasted Mrs. Billingsworth's snow cake, Clemma?" Her older sister, Caroline, flush with the expectancy of a fourth child, appeared at her side as the exhibition began. She pressed a small plate at Clemma. "It is ever so delicious! I believe Mrs. Billingsworth must have used the best Bermuda arrowroot, for honestly, this cake is so light! It has a lemon flavor, and you know how utterly I adore lemon."

Clemma took the plate and managed to swallow a bite of cake. "Indeed, it is superb."

"And Mrs. Plummer has brought the most heavenly white gingerbread. Dear me, I fear I shall be fatter than ever!"

"You are hardly fat, Caroline."

"No, I suppose not, for I am quite sure that I am as lovely as ever I was. Do you not agree that this lavender gown looks well on me, Clemma? I believe it brings out the blue in my eyes."

"They are looking quite blue tonight."

"I knew it! I told my dear husband how very blue I thought my eyes appeared in this shade of lavender, and he said, 'Eyes are eyes, and that is that.' Can you imagine? Such a dullard. It is a wonder we are so happy together. But we are, for you know he allows me to buy any sort of fabric I like, even the newest patterns from London, and I can wear any color I wish. And do you not think my hair is artfully arranged, dear Clemma? See how it loops just so in the back?"

Clemma dutifully examined and admired the loops in her sister's hair. But she could not find it in herself to rejoice overmuch in Caroline's beauty. Her heart felt heavy in her chest, she realized as the festivities got under way and guests came and went.

It was not the exhibition that dispirited her. No, the hall was awash with Christmas joy. Swags of fir branches tied with bright red ribbons hung from the stair rails and chandeliers. White beeswax candles cast a golden glow about the hall. The aroma of freshly baked cakes and sweets filled the air, mingling with the luxurious scent of hot apple cider spiced with cloves. And the cheerful chatter interspersed with hearty congratulations should have been enough to lift even the glummest of spirits.

Nor was it the problematic Christmas Rose that had discouraged Clemma. She knew her paintings were notable, a supreme expression of her talent. If she wished to be recognized for her art, she could not have put forth a better effort.

It was not even the usual loneliness she felt at this season. On special occasions, she often missed her husband and mourned the family she might have had. This Christmas Eve, she remembered him wistfully. But time had eased the sharpness of her loss, and she had long ago surrendered any hope of children or a home of her own.

No, the weight that beset her had to do with the absence of one particular guest. Dr. Paul Baine had not made an appearance in the church hall, though Clemma had sent him a printed invitation and had even handwritten a plea for his presence. He would not come. He did not feel welcome in church. He knew the villagers still hated and feared him. Clemma had not been able to bring herself to return to Nasmyth Manor following their conversation at teatime. How could she face him alone again? How could she enter his house, knowing he loved her—and knowing how deeply she loved him— yet certain there could be no union between them?

No, it was best that she never set foot in Nasmyth Manor again. And best that he not come to her exhibition. Yet, how she missed him! How she longed for him!

"Clemma, I must speak to you concerning a matter of great import!" Her sister Madeline stepped to her side. "Mama has just told me the most appalling piece of news. I can hardly credit it, yet I fear it must be true. Oh, tell me it is not true, dear Clemma, for how shall we endure it?"

"Endure what, Maddie? Speak plainly, I beg you."

"Mama has told me that you invited . . . you

invited . . . oh, I can hardly bring myself to speak his name."

"Dr. Baine? Yes, I did invite him. He is my friend."

"Clementine Laird, you ought to be ashamed of yourself! Mama tells me you have been going almost daily to that . . . that awful place—"

"Nasmyth Manor."

"How can you speak the name so lightly? Dear Clemma, please tell me you have not sunk so low in society as to befriend a man like that! I shall tell Caroline what has happened. She and I, together with our husbands, shall bring you out into good company again. We shall find you better companions. We shall introduce you to our friends, and you will marry someone who—"

"No, Maddie!" Clemma said. "I shall not marry. You forget yourself."

Maddie stared at her, her face turning pink and then red and then white again. "Oh, I know you cannot marry, but Clemma really, you must not associate with such a man as that . . . that—"

"Paul Baine. For heaven's sake, Madeline, he is not the devil. He is, in fact, a very good and generous and kind—"

"Oh, spare us! Save us from condemnation! Dear Clemma, he has come!"

"What?" Clemma turned to the door to find

that Paul Baine had just stepped into the church hall and was brushing snowflakes from his top hat. At the sight of him, an unexpected joy flooded her chest, a shiver ran down her spine, and she clasped her hands together in delight.

"Paul! He is here." Rushing forward, she nearly ran into Mr. Street, the London book dealer who was intently examining August. "Welcome, Dr. Baine!" she cried as she neared him. "I am so very glad to see you!"

Spotting her, he straightened, and his face broke into a smile. "Mrs. Laird, how lovely you look this evening."

Clemma could have danced a jig, she felt so light and happy. Picking up the burgundy velvet skirts of her new Christmas gown, she ran the last few steps toward him.

But just as she reached him, the mayor stepped between them. "Dr. Baine," he said. "I am surprised to find you here."

"I was invited to the exhibition," Paul said. He drew his invitation from his coat pocket. "I am a guest of the artist, in fact."

"And yet I find it unseemly that you should mingle in this company. We are gathered here for a celebration. I cannot believe that any reminder of the sin and evil that plague this world is welcome."

Clemma caught her breath in horror at the

words she knew she herself might have spoken only a month before.

Paul stared stonily at the mayor. Then he stepped to one side. "I was invited," he repeated. "I am a guest of the hostess."

"Mrs. Laird." The Reverend Springle caught her elbow and leaned forward to whisper in her ear. "Did you invite this man? Surely this is a mistake. Dr. Baine is a man of very low moral character."

Clemma swallowed hard. She could see Madeline and Caroline nearly wilting beside the cider bowl. Mama was fanning herself so hard that her ringlets had begun to dance. And Papa seemed to be mumbling a lengthy quotation from Milton. Dare she further embarrass and humiliate them? Dare she set herself apart from her family and the good society that had been her world all her life?

"Mrs. Laird," Reverend Springle continued, "truly, I believe a man of such ill repute must not defile these hallowed halls. May I ask you to send him away for the sake of the good company gathered here to celebrate this occasion with you?"

Clemma looked around her at the villagers who loved her so dearly—women who had baked cakes and pressed apples into cider for her. Men who had chopped evergreen branches and hung her paintings. Boys who had draped the fir swags around the hall, and girls who had covered the tables in white cloths and had lit the candles.

"Dr. Baine does not belong among us, Mrs. Laird," the mayor said. "I have heard rumors of your worthy efforts to influence him, but madam, I assure you that a man such as he has no place in this gathering. He is not wanted."

Clemma looked into Paul Baine's eyes and saw the utter resignation he felt as he replaced his top hat and began to wrap his scarf around his neck. But as he turned to go, she spoke up.

"'When thou makest a dinner or a supper,'" she said, repeating Scripture that Papa had made her memorize, "'call not thy friends, nor thy brethren, neither thy kinsmen, nor thy rich neighbours. . . . But when thou makest a feast, call the poor, the maimed, the lame, the blind: And thou shalt be blessed.'"

The mayor looked at the minister. And then Reverend Springle cleared his throat. "Yes, indeed, Mrs. Laird," he said. "That is quite right. But this man is not physically corrupted. It is his spirit that is black, dear lady. The Bible makes it quite clear that good Christians are not to spend time in the company of evildoers. 'Blessed is the man that walketh not in the counsel of the ungodly, nor standeth in the way of sinners, nor sitteth in the seat of—'"

"'If ye love them which love you, what thank have

ye?'" Clemma returned, anguish twisting her voice.
"'But love ye your enemies, and do good.'"

"Dear Clemma," Mama spoke up, hurrying
toward her daughter. "You must listen to Reverend
Springle."

"'Be ye therefore merciful, as your Father also is
merciful,'" Clemma continued, unable to stop the
tears that trickled down her cheeks. "'Judge not,
and ye shall not be judged: condemn not, and ye
shall not be condemned—'"

"Clemma," Paul said. "It is all right. I shall go."

"No!" She grabbed his hand as she faced those
gathered about her. "'Forgive, and ye shall be
forgiven.' Reverend Springle, you know these words
as well as I do. You have spoken them many times
from your pulpit. And yet now, when faced with a
man you consider ungodly, you condemn him, and
judge him, and refuse to forgive him."

"Well, yes, but I . . . but he . . ."

"What do you know of Paul Baine, Mama and
Papa? He is a worthy gentleman. His home is filled
with the ill and needy. His hands are busy with healing and love. I have been to Nasmyth Manor, and I
have seen the change in Dr. Baine. But even if he
had not changed, he should find sanctuary here—in
the church of all places! Please, I beg you to make
him as comfortable and easy as you make me."

Amid the stunned silence, Paul Baine removed

his hat once again. "Perhaps it would be well if I spoke for just a moment. The words Mrs. Laird have spoken about me are true. I have changed. Yet I wish to say now to her, even more than to the good people gathered in this place, that my motives in making these changes were misguided. I believed that by ceasing my previous practices and by instead using my skills for healing and preserving life, I might please God well enough to be forgiven."

He paused and took both her hands in his before continuing. "With your help, Mrs. Laird, I now understand that God's forgiveness is not something I can earn. It is a gift, paid for by the blood of Christ, whose words were quoted earlier. May I now publicly state that I wish to accept this free gift? I realize it may make no difference to your society, Mrs. Laird, that I have changed my ways or that I have surrendered my life and my future into the hands of God. Yet, to me, it is everything. And I thank you, Mrs. Laird . . . beautiful Clementine . . . for showing me the face of Jesus."

With a crisp bow, he turned and left the church.

SIX

"WHAT A GLORIOUS EVENING!" Papa said as the carriage bore the family through the snow toward Brooking House. "My dear Clementine, you shone like a bright jewel at your exhibition tonight."

"Indeed, I am still trembling," Mama added in a weak voice. "To think . . . to imagine that you . . . that Mr. Street came all the way from London to Otley, and that he would . . . oh, it is too much!"

"It is certainly not too much, Mrs. Bowden," Papa said. "Why should our daughter not be asked to illustrate the royal Christmas card for the coming year?"

"But the queen, Mr. Bowden. Queen Victoria herself! The very idea that our little Clemma's paintings would be sent out across the empire—"

"Not my paintings, Mama," Clemma clarified. "Mr. Street would make a print of one work of art. He prints all sorts of cards for Queen Victoria."

"The Queen of England! Oh, do you hear how it sounds, husband? Our daughter is to paint the queen's Christmas card. It is too wonderful! Really, it is far too wonderful!"

"I believe Clemma would have been happier if Mr. Street had wanted to print a book of her Yorkshire flowers exhibition. That was your dream, was it not, dear girl?"

"Yes, Papa, but the Christmas card will make a fine introduction into the London art world."

"Perhaps you will show your Yorkshire flowers at the Tate Gallery one day," Mama said. "Can you imagine that? We must bring Caroline and Madeline, of course, and the grandchildren. And perhaps our darling Ivy will have come home to us by then. We miss her terribly, do we not, Mr. Bowden? It hardly seems like Christmas without Ivy. And we shall all want new gowns for the exhibition. I am certain Caroline will have several innovative ideas for the seamstresses in Leeds. Can you imagine how excited she will be to think of attending an exhibit at the Tate Gallery in London?"

"I should think she will be jealous over Clemma's invitation to meet Queen Victoria herself." Papa beamed at his youngest daughter.

"For no doubt you will be asked to attend court, my dear. Once the queen has seen your illustration, she will insist upon meeting you. Think of the gowns we shall have to produce for that occasion."

Clemma smiled as her focus wandered to the snow-blanketed dales and fells outside the carriage window. "I can hardly think beyond the painting I must execute, Papa. How shall I arrange the bouquet? And what foliage should I feature?"

"Holly," Mama said immediately. "I am so fond of holly at Christmastime. Mistletoe would be nice as well."

"Mistletoe is a blasted nuisance!" Papa exclaimed. "It is a pest of the worst order."

"Nonsense. It is lovely!"

While her parents discussed the merits and detriments of the various plants associated with the season, Clemma recalled the stubborn Christmas Rose that had refused to bloom. Perhaps one day it would blossom, a beautiful flower emerging from a dark, poisonous root. With that image, her thoughts drifted to Paul Baine . . . how dark his own life had been and how bright the promise of his future. But somehow the prospect did not ease the heaviness in her heart.

As the carriage passed the gates to Longley Park, Clemma's focus lingered on the white-capped outline of the great manor, the faint silhouette of the carriage house, the geometric pattern of the hedge maze cloaked in snow. But when her gaze arrived at the great glass conservatory, she drew in a gasp of surprise.

"There is a light in the conservatory!" she said. "Someone has left a candle burning."

"Oh, dear! And on Christmas Eve," Mama cried. "It will burn right down and start a fire."

"Now, then, Mrs. Bowden, do not upset your daughter by speaking of fires." Papa reached over and patted Clemma's hand. "It will be all right, my dear."

"No, Papa, please, you must stop the carriage. I cannot bear to think of losing the conservatory."

"Indeed, Mr. Bowden, Clemma goes there nearly every day. It would be too hard on her to lose it."

"It is not me, Mama. It is the plants. They will suffer so and be ruined. And the wicker tea tables will burn up. And the glass will be stained with smoke. Oh, please, Papa!"

He was already calling out the window to the driver, and in moments the carriage had pulled through the gates on its way down the long drive toward the conservatory.

"Perhaps one of the Longley art students is inside," Papa conjectured. "I should think the moonlight on the palm trees might inspire a painting of wildest Africa."

"But it is Christmas Eve," Clemma said. "The art students have all gone home. Mr. Hedgley sometimes checks the doors, but he and his wife attended the exhibition almost until the last moment. I cannot think who . . ." She faltered, suddenly realizing that she did know exactly who had lit the candle inside the conservatory.

"It is Dr. Baine," she whispered, as the carriage pulled to a stop near the looming glass structure.

"Dr. Baine?" Mama said. "But why would he visit the conservatory at this hour?"

"Because he knows I will not be there."

"Then you must not go inside, my dear. Leave him to his reveries."

"Mama, I need to see him. I need to be with him."

"Clementine, dearest girl, he is not the man for you. Certainly your father and I have accepted the friendship you offered him. We believe, as you told us, that he is changed. But it is clear that he feels . . . that his desire is for more than friendship. Clemma, I fear he loves you."

"He does love me, Mama. And I love him." She bowed her head. "But you need not concern yourself about our love. You know as well as I that nothing . . . that he . . . that we could never . . ."

As she began to weep, Papa drew her into his embrace. "Go and greet him, my dear. Invite him to dinner tomorrow at Brooking House."

"And tell him to bring Mary Elizabeth," Mama added. "I am longing to hold a baby again, and I shall not be able to do so until Caroline delivers, which is ever so long from now."

"Four months," Papa said. "My grandson will arrive with the tulips."

As they debated the relative length of time until their next grandchild was born, Clemma slipped out of the carriage. Though a path had been cleared, the newly fallen snow chilled her feet as she made her way to the door. When she stepped into the vast green warmth of the conservatory, she let her hood fall back onto her shoulders. She should remove her heavy wool cloak, she realized, but now she could see Paul sitting on a wicker settee near her easel, and she hurried toward him.

"Dr. Baine," she called softly. "We saw the light from our carriage."

Clearly surprised, he stood quickly. "Mrs. Laird."

"Clemma."

"I did not expect you."

"No, but I have come."

He gazed at her, his chest rising and falling with the labor of his breath. And then he closed the space between them in two strides and caught her in his arms.

"Clemma, my darling, my beautiful love!" His lips met hers, and she melted into his kiss. "I have sat here for hours trying to believe there can be no future for us, and I cannot accept it. I cannot imagine my life without you. Clemma, I love you. I have loved you from the moment we met."

"But on the day we met, I charged you five pounds for an orange!"

He laughed and his arms tightened around her. "It is that very spirit, that determination and stubbornness, which I love so much! This quality in you has brought me to healing. Clemma, please say you have not come here on another mission of salvation—not unless that mission is to save me from an empty lifetime of loving you, wanting you, needing you as my wife."

"Oh, Paul!" As his lips covered hers again, Clemma slipped her hands around the breadth of his back, absorbing the rough texture of his wool coat and the strength of the muscle beneath it. How could she bear to part from him? And yet, the impossibility of their love tore through her.

"I love you, Paul," she cried as his lips grazed her ear, her cheek, the side of her neck. "I love you. I wish I could . . . I wish . . . oh, Paul, my dearest love . . ."

"Clemma, why are you weeping? Please tell me what troubles you."

"I cannot!"

"You must. I insist upon it." With one finger,

he tilted her chin and forced her to look into his eyes. "You know everything about me—every sin, every degradation, every failing. Please, I beg you, tell me now what it is that holds you back."

"It is not you."

"Then what is it?"

"Me!" she cried, searching hopelessly for her handkerchief. How could she tell him? How could she reveal this terrible secret known only to herself and her family?

"Clemma, I love you. Nothing you can say will change that." He cradled her head in the hollow of his neck. "Dearest girl, you have been such an example to me of God and his undeserved forgiveness. Let me now be to you an example of his unconditional love."

Choking down a ragged breath, she nodded. "I am . . . I am not beautiful. I am not . . . I am not fully a woman."

He took her shoulders and looked into her eyes. "What do you mean by this? Speak plainly."

"In the fire, the fire that killed my husband and destroyed our home, I was injured. My body . . . my female form . . . a flaming beam fell upon me, trapping me for a time until I was able to drag myself from beneath it. But the damage was done. What you see of me—my face—is all that was not scarred."

"Clemma, I am so sorry!"

She bit her lip, trying not to cry again. "The beam fell across me at an angle." She demonstrated, drawing a line from one shoulder to the opposite hip. "This part of my flesh . . . all of it . . . was burned away."

He said nothing for a moment, his eyes searching her face, his hands tight on her shoulders. "You are telling me that your bosom was destroyed," he said.

She looked away, heat flowing into her cheeks. "Partially. And my flesh is hideously scarred. I am malformed."

Certain he would reject her now, she attempted to pull away. But he refused to release her, instead drawing her close again. His arms slipped around her and his cheek pressed against hers.

"Clemma, my beautiful love," he whispered. "I am a doctor, my darling. I have seen the ravages of illness and injury upon the human body. Nothing about you can ever disgust or repulse me."

"But you have not seen—"

"I do not need to see in order to know that what I say is true. Clemma, it is not your body that draws me. Though I am a man, and I desire the full joy of marriage, I have not founded my love for you upon the promise of a fine figure or unscathed skin. You must believe me when I tell you that I love you, and I will always love you, no matter how you appear."

Hardly able to fathom the truth of his words, she gave in hopelessly to the tears that spilled down her cheeks.

"I am ugly!" she ground out. "I am hideous!"

"You are beautiful."

"No!"

"Clemma, do you love me?"

"Yes, Paul, but—"

"You love me even though you know that my soul is scarred from the sin that beset me?"

"I do."

"Then allow me to love you despite the fire that ravaged your body. I am whole on the outside but scarred within. You are scarred on the outside but beautiful within. Clemma, together we make a whole creature—a beautiful, forgiven, loved, and accepted whole! Believe that, I beg you."

"Oh, Paul, how I long to know that what you say is true. Yet I have spent so many years protecting myself from any exposure. I have always known that a man could never love me. That my body would repel him. That the marriage bed would become a thing of horror."

"Let me see," he said. "Remove your cloak, Clemma. Allow me to see the scars."

"Paul!" The very idea appalled her. But he reached for the clasp that held her cloak, and in a moment it fell away. Then his hand rose to her shoulder and covered the loose neck of her velvet evening gown. She stiffened, trembling in dismay, as he slid the fabric to one side and exposed the discolored skin beneath it.

"I love you, Clemma," he said, running one finger over her scarred shoulder. Then he bent and kissed it. "I love this shoulder, my darling. And I will love every other part of you with the same devotion."

"You are not . . . not horrified?"

He smiled. "I am enchanted by the mystery of you. I am intrigued by your secrets. I am beguiled by your charms. There is nothing . . . certainly not this well-guarded secret of yours . . . that can make me love you less than I do at this moment. And if you will consent to be my wife, Clemma, I know that my love for you will grow stronger and more enduring with each passing day."

"Can this be so?"

"It is so. It will be so if only you will agree to marry me. Say it, Clemma. Say you will become my wife."

"Oh, Paul, of course I will!" She threw her arms around his neck, laughter and disbelief mingling with her tears. "I love you so much, my darling! I long to spend my life with you. I long to become the mother of little Mary Elizabeth and—if God is willing—the children that I shall bear you."

"Children!" he cried, lifting her high and twirling her around and around. "A family!"

"A home!" she called out, with a little shriek of delight. "A husband! Oh, thank you, God! I could not even bring myself to pray for such a gift—and yet you have given it to me."

"And I have another heaven-sent gift to show you, my dearest Clemma," Paul said, setting her down gently. "Come with me."

Taking her hand, he drew her down the path to a small marble pedestal on which sat a forlorn little clay pot. He held the candle close to the evergreen leaves and gestured for Clemma to have a look.

"A bud!" she cried. "The Christmas Rose is budding!"

"Before long, you will have a bloom to paint."

"Just in time for Queen Victoria's Christmas card."

"The queen's Christmas card?" he asked. "Clemma, what—"

"Oh, life is too wonderful! My blessings are more than I can count!" Standing on tiptoe, she kissed his cheek. "Come and ask Papa for my hand in marriage, Paul, for he will give it gladly. He and Mama wait in the carriage. They will be so happy to learn that no matter how black the root, indeed, a young bud always lies sleeping. And one day, even in the most stubborn of plants, there will bloom a flower upon the Christmas Rose!"

ABOUT THE AUTHOR

CATHERINE PALMER'S FIRST BOOK was published in
1988, and since then she has published nearly thirty
books with Crown, Bantam, Silhouette, Berkley,
and Tyndale House. Combined sales of all her
books number more than one million copies.

Catherine's first hardcover novel, *The Happy Room*,
debuted earlier this year to critical acclaim. Her
suspense novel, *A Dangerous Silence*, is a CBA best-
seller, and her HeartQuest book *A Touch of Betrayal*
won the 2001 Christy Award (Romance category).
Her novella "Under His Wings," which appears in
the anthology *A Victorian Christmas Cottage*, was named
Northern Lights Best Novella of 1999 (Historical
category) by Midwest Fiction Writers. Her numer-

ous other awards include Best Historical Romance, Best Contemporary Romance, and Best of Romance from the Southwest Writers Workshop; Most Exotic Historical Romance Novel from *Romantic Times* magazine; and Best Historical Romance Novel from Romance Writers of the Panhandle.

Catherine lives in Missouri with her husband, Tim, and sons, Geoffrey and Andrei. She has degrees from Baylor University and Southwest Baptist University.

BOOKS BY
CATHERINE PALMER

English Ivy
The Happy Room
A Dangerous Silence
A Touch of Betrayal—winner of the 2001 Christy Award
A Kiss of Adventure (original title: *The Treasure of Timbuktu*)
A Whisper of Danger (original title: *The Treasure of Zanzibar*)
Finders Keepers
Hide & Seek
Prairie Rose
Prairie Fire
Prairie Storm

ANTHOLOGIES:

A Victorian Christmas Keepsake
A Victorian Christmas Cottage
A Victorian Christmas Quilt
A Victorian Christmas Tea
Prairie Christmas